SILVER CHRONICLES

THE BLOOD CHIMERA

BIANCA TAYLOR

Branches of Arcana

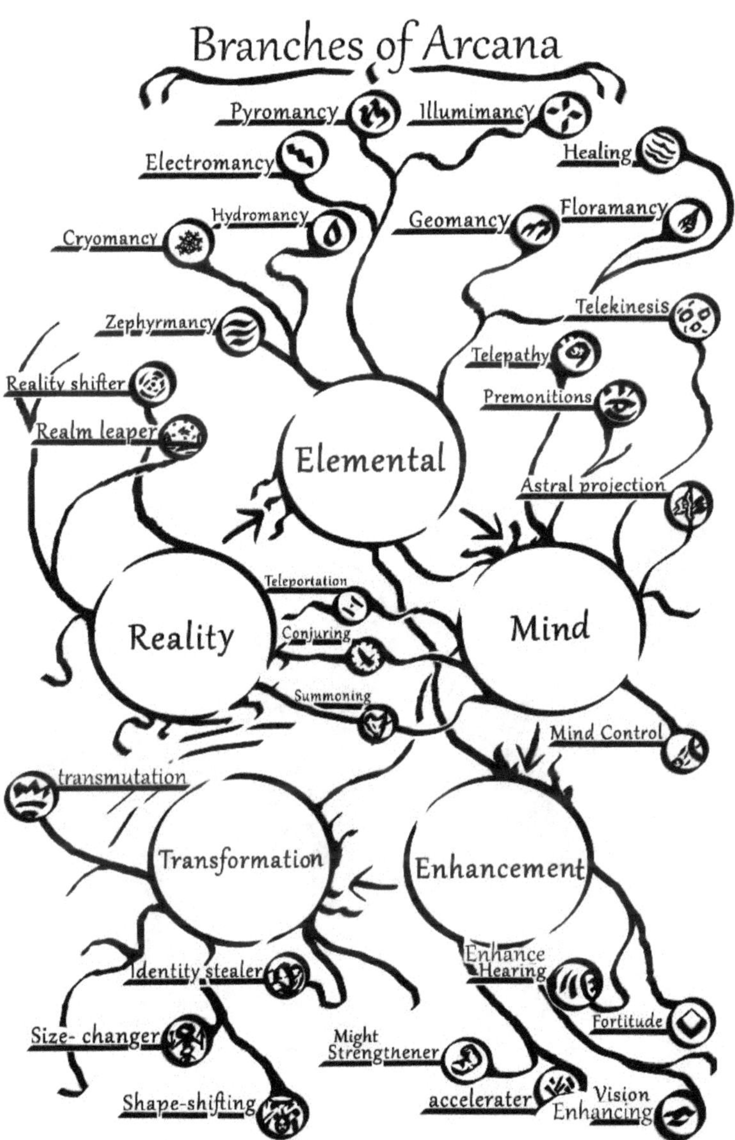

CONTENTS

PROLOGUE
Centuries

From a tale told by Oran Glynn,
an
knowledgeable sorcerer from the Thiar Realm

Come young and old, come closer. Sit on my knee or here… right next to me. I, the great master sorcerer of old, have a tale to tell. One that is new to most and mostly forgotten by the few who saw it all happen. Let this old sage lay before your ears and enquiring eyes the story of the ages and ages before now, in the distant past. My calling is to feed your heart, rub your ears, and wipe open your eyes.

So, come. Yes, reach out and listen carefully to this old grey beard. I have the tale of tales to tell. Now…

As the tale goes, in a past long gone, there was a time when all thirteen known realms were connected, open to travel between them freely. Then, all things changed suddenly when the war of the rogue divines against all mortal races began. They saw the growth of the magical powers of the mortals reaching their own levels. Feeling threatened by this development, two of the four great divines, higher beings of great power, Abyzias, the divine of ocean and ice, along with Cthithanis, the divine of darkness and fear, with Zilvagron, the divine of flora and the wild, lead an army of a hundred lesser immortals.

So they went on their crusade of death. The other two divines were against it, still allowing this to happen as they did not wish to interfere in the struggles of mortals. As the war raged on for over two centuries and the mortal races struggled against the onslaught, the immortal foes could not be slain.

It was looking grim; their chances of survival were woefully slim.

The tide changed when a miracle happened! A great elven sorcerer and innovator of magic, known as Valo Munari, discovered a way to steal the power of the divines and their followers and contain it, divided into two black steel chests. With this new knowledge, they set a trap for the rogue divine army and, after a heroic battle, emerged victorious from the war.

The rogue divines and their army scattered across the known realms, mere husks of their former selves, wandering across those realms… powerless. Half of their extracted powers had been locked away underneath the palace in the capital of the elven realm. The key was in the form of a winding crimson marking on the arm of the keeper. The current reigning ruler of the realm holds the key as a show of appreciation for their significant contribution to the war's end.

The other half of the divine's powers were given to the leader of the divines, his key, a cobalt amulet embedded on his chest, who had kept out of the conflict, namely Haulgio, the sun divine, along with the remaining three divines, who did not rebel. This ensured the powers were safely kept away from the rogue divines and any attempts to reclaim them. The magic-elven knowledge of the secret to extract and contain these powers was destroyed as per the resolution reached with Haulgio to prevent more conflict with the divines and ensure good relations with them.

Still, the scars of the war lingered even decades later, and the known realms were considerably more dangerous places than before.

Hurt and desperate people turned to violence and theft. Certain realms were hit harder. So, over the following decades, slowly, each realm decided to cut themselves off from the rest of the realms to protect and rebuild their own worlds. Travel between the realms was forbidden altogether - taking away and destroying the portals leading between realms. Some kept their worlds open longer, yet in the end, everyone followed. Now, the realms are separated, no longer interacting with each other as in the days of old, as it still is. A tense, dark gloom hangs over these broken and divided worlds.

Still, one can but wonder if this divide shall remain forever or will it as all things change, as change always does... and could this change be for the better or worse of the realms... and what events will cause this change?.... That is a question I will tell you, my dear listener, as I was involved with it.

CHAPTER 1
Hunting Sulfrens

At the outskirts of the Severne realms.

Near the bottom of a towering cliff. In front of a deserted crumbling structure made of dark obsidian stone, an ancient forgotten temple, stands the elven King Eilif Solstris. The sun shines on his long, light blonde hair with two braids in front of each pointed ear. He usually does not go to such places. These parts are the favored lair of a powerful creature, often spotted lurking within, one of the beasts created and unleashed during the divine war, known as sulfrens.

There are still a few clusters of them left in the realm, even after two hundred years, and getting him to show up personally is not an easy feat, as he won't just show up to slay any monster. These sightings included a mention of a titan sulfren among them, a blue-eyed thunder variant. Recognized as one of the most powerful beasts across the ages…. a beast that will require vast arcane capabilities to defeat, as he has.

Looking straight toward the entrance with his mint green eyes, he moves ahead into the structure, into the dark passage dimly lit by smoky flickering torches against the cracked walls. His personal elite guards, the Crows, are a group of four powerful fighters. They have gone ahead to survey the area.

Walking through the wide passage, his florentine patterned cape, embroidered with celestial blue flames, elegantly flows behind him. The side of his fair face covered by a shadow from the grey fur collar of his cape, his silvery white doublet underneath it, he strides with confident caution.

As he goes even deeper into the ruin, Eilif studies the stone walls as he passes, adorned with a vast stone carved mural depicting immense creatures hovering over a mountain range, some serpentine, some draconic, and even some otherworldly-monstrous in their appearance. They are fighting against giant humanoid beings radiating energy.
Fascinating, but he has more pressing matters to attend to, a monster to stop.

He moves on through the slightly lit path, listening intently to the distant screeching noises of the beast, echoing, echoing, echoing … as he gets nearer to the center.

A slim muscular figure uniformed in the garb the Crow wear steps forward to meet the King: a long-hooded forest green coat, a dark metal cuirass breastplate with light grey leaf detailing, grey metallic gloves, and a black steel mask with grey markings, shaped to resemble the face of a crow.

Wearing an arcane weapon made for the King's elite guard, this warrior is equipped with a bronze rapier hanging from his belt embedded with an amethyst at its hilt's end, for each Crow's sword holds a different gem, each made from another metal. Each is skilled in their own form of combat magic, and each has its own code name.

In front of a broken and torn open door, the Crow stands watching Eilif come closer. Doing a quick bow as he sees his King, he addresses him respectfully. "Your Highness, I awaited your arrival."

The Crow then continues to explain the situation. "Nightshade, Larkspur, and Nerium have positioned themselves in the inner chamber, where the six sulfrens are prowling about. They await your command to attack, hidden in the shadows, avoiding the beast's detection." Looking past the Crow, Eilif instructs: "Lead the way then, Wolfsbane." Pausing his sentence, a deep anger shows on his visage as he continues: "I shall face the titan sulfren, while you and the other Crows shall recon with the others. Keeping them out of my way, understood." Giving a slight nod, Wolfsbane replies. "As you wish, Your Highness, we shall fight by your side." The Crow strolls toward the broken door as he finishes his words, Eilif following behind. They enter into a grand hall. Large, damaged spiraling obsidian pillars, with torn jade green banners brandishing a silver stag head embroidered into it, hanging between each. They pass through to the next door, to their objective.

Inside a sizeable octagonal-shaped chamber filled with piles of debris scattered all over, the beasts known as the sulfrens roam in the center, screeching and growling, scratching at the stone floor. They appear as giant wolves with pale scales instead of fur, glowing purple tendrils across their backs, and a skinny, long tail. Eyes completely black with tiny purple dots, staring intently at the floor, digging with their elongated clawed paws. A gigantic one lies down next to the pack. The titan sulfren. He shares the other scaly white body and glowing purple tendrils but is much bulkier, with reddish black spikes running down his spine and four massive purple-colored horns in front of his face with a pair of glowing blue eyes. Along with red markings all over his body.

Hiding behind a giant pile of broken black stones near the chamber's entrance, two Crows crouch with another watching from a high ledge above them.

One of the Crows remarks while observing the sulfrens. She is the newest member of their group, a replacement for the previous deceased Nerium, inheriting his codename and clothing. "What do you think they are digging for? I swear, whenever we find these monsters, they're busy searching intently for something. Mostly with a titan watching over them…. Nightshade…. Nightshade?" Nerium whispers to her fellow Crow warrior, who crouched behind her with his hand resting on a platinum sword with an Aquamarine on the end of its hilt. "That doesn't matter. Our job here is to stop a threat, not to analyze how these monsters act and why." He tells her, annoyed that she asked him in the first place.

Pointing angrily with her brass sword embedded with a garnet at Nightshade. "You're seriously not even a bit curious at all. Shouldn't we know what they are doing in case it is realm-threatening and not just some strange behavior?" She asks, with a quiet but angry tone. "No, not at all. Never crossed my mind in the slightest…. All I need to know is where they are so I can do my duty to kill these things," He bluntly responds, angering her more. Standing up, she readies her argument but is interrupted.

As the third Crow stationed there, Larkspur, lands lightly between them from above, startling Nerium, who steps back in surprise. Larkspur Stands up, shaking off the dust from his uniform: "You two better stop your trivial bickering; I can sense Wolfsbane and King Eilif are going to come through the door." He says, glaring strictly at Nerium and Nightshade… intensely disappointed in their lack of professionalism, arguing like this when they came here to accomplish a crucial task…. he just doesn't understand them as one who takes everything he does as something of great importance. "I don't think he would approve of his elite guard arguing like a couple of children." He adds as he focuses his gaze on the door. Both of them reluctantly answer, "Fine." Nerium says, clearly still frustrated with all of this… while Nightshade just nods in answer to it.

Entering the chamber. The King walks in first, and Wolfsbane goes past him and takes his position next to the other Crows. Having fought with the King before on rare occasions when a titan sulfren appeared, they knew exactly what they had to do. Holding his hand up, showing a sign to his fellow, the Crow to ready themselves to commence the attack. "Nerium, Nightshade, go right to the back; I shall go in from the front with Larkspur and Wolfsbane, encircling the sulfren pack." Eilif speaks out his command with authority, wasting no time with small details. Each takes out their weapon, moving out in all directions to their attack positions.

King Eilif runs toward the rubble with Wolfsbane and Larkspur, Leaping across the giant heap of broken stone. This instantly alerts the beastly sulfrens, making them charge violently, filling the ruins with their terrible wild screeching.

The other Crows take on the smaller sulfrens, two from the back and two from the front. Attacking swiftly. Using their weapons to channel their manna to fight back with various spells.

Walking past them with determination in his eyes - straight to his target, the King armed with a pair of glistening razor-sharp golden chakram disks engraved with a fiery pattern with obsidian embedded around black flames being produced from it, hovering slightly over his palms.

Launching it forward, spinning at high velocity, enveloped by black flames. Heading toward the titan that is barrelling at Eilif with a thundering screech!

CHAPTER 2
Mastering a powerful spell

Far away from the outskirts, where Eilif and the Crows are fighting the beasts, at the capital of the realm. As the sun begins to set glowingly upon the cold land, the dazzling marble castle known as the Hyvits Palace, with its elegantly soaring spires, stands proudly surrounded by lofty, snowy mountain peaks. The city of Tulifyr sprawls out beneath its splendor and beyond the great forest that encircles the capital, like an evergreen carpet draped over the foothills of the majestic ranges. The elven capital's residents and the palace's inhabitants slow down and settle for the night.

One of them remains alert outside, next to the palace's walls. Crouched beneath its looming shadow, he works diligently, trying to perfect a spell he has worked on for many moons. Prince Atgeir Solstris has chosen to stay out tonight to work on a highly complicated spell… alone and out of sight. He despises being seen to fail at anything, as his pride is too great.

Holding both hands together from underneath his indigo blue cloak, in front of his body, suited with silver clawed gauntlets embedded with a single bloodstone each, he focuses his thoughts and mana at a single point between his palms. A small crimson ball of electricity forms, illuminating his fair skin. A scar created by a vicious claw during a past incident in his childhood, lurks underneath his Azure blue eyes. Grinning wide with satisfaction, he tries to expand the ball further. The crackling ball gradually grows as he slowly expands the space between his hands.

Now for the hard part, he failed every time before. He starts to close his hands again, trying to compress the crackling ball of mana energy while not noticing the pair of eyes watching him from behind a wall.

As the scarlet ball of lightning compresses to the size of a tangerine, he observes it closely … it appears stable. "Perfect!" he exclaims as he moves it to the palm of one hand, and Atgeir stands poised to launch it towards a target he marked on a nearby tree.

It all seems as if it is going to work, and then suddenly:

Boom!

The Scarlet orb explodes next to his face, and the escaping projectile of brilliant mana power launches straight into the hard stone wall, bursting into a dazzle of sparks!

Laying flat on his back, Atgeir loudly curses while clutching his hand, searing with pain. He hears someone running towards him.

Still dazed by the explosion, he hastily stumbles onto his feet, dusting himself off and trying to comb back his hair. With his gauntlet, he quickly collects his long waist-length jet-black hair into a neat low ponytail, dusting off his regal white attire adorned with golden trimmings. Nobody may see him out of sorts!

As the figure approaches, shouting out loudly in concern as they approach, he sees it is just his little sister, the youngest in the family. The overly concerned and caring Aada. Ran toward him, holding her long white and grey dress tight to avoid tripping.
Coming to a hasty halt before him, she examines him with distress in her light green eyes, wide in her pleasant face, framed by short golden blonde hair. "Uhh…Atgeir …. Atgeir, are you fine?.... No serious injuries or anything?" She tries to check his head but gets pushed aside by him. "Of course, I am fine; you know who you are talking about - it's me, and I am perfectly fine." He responds, slightly annoyed. She backs up a bit, giving him some room.
"That's good." She says, relieved. "Though you should have told someone before preparing for tomorrow's test match with Fath…" She is interrupted by Atgeir.

"And what are you doing out here? Did you seriously just follow me here?" He tries to remain relaxed but is still much annoyed at her. She hastily talks: "I can explain that. I was going to ask something earlier today, then I saw you sneaking outside and…"

He interrupts her again.

"Fine... fine…. just don't tell about anything you saw here to mother or father or anyone for that matter, Aada." A grin spreads on his face before continuing his sentence. "Or I will tell your little secret, you know, that you tripped into that precious ancient tapestry hanging in the great hall and tore it." She gulps loudly in fear at his words." Wouldn't he punish you by sending you to the archive for an entire fortnight, going through dusty manuscripts with old Vilho? Do you really wish to spend your time down there?" He elaborates to her further, as Aada quickly cuts in, "It was an acci…... fine, I won't tell." She nervously promises. "Like I would have told them in the first place." She adds under her breath and folds her arms obstinately.

Atgeir looks smugly down on her. "Now that is agreed upon. You should go back into the palace." He states. She responds weakly, staring down at her feet. "Fine… I will leave; I could have helped with your training." She starts to walk away. "Stop." He calls out to her, and her face lightens up, hoping he changes his mind. "I'm coming with you to ensure you actually leave." He clarifies as she turns towards him, her hopes dashed at his statement. She slouches a bit as she gives a weak sigh. "Right."

Looking back a moment, Atgeir looks back at the trees behind him. A slight look of disdain appears in his eyes at something in the shadows. Looking hastily back upon the palace.

As he strides past her with his head held up high. Aada just reluctantly falls in behind him, walking hastily behind him.

Hidden in the shadows.

As they walk back toward the palace doors, far out of their field of view, hiding behind foliage in the gardens, Thyra sits, crouched, looking on. She is the other younger sister, the second youngest, the constantly forgotten and ignored one of the four. A thing about herself, she has learned to just…. not care about anymore.

Thyra can tell Atgeir clearly spotted her there but did not even bother to come over and expose that she was hiding there.

She just watches them leave; she does not bother going towards them to show herself to them. They treat her so cruelly because they consider her cursed: anyone who comes too close to her gets their mana slowly drained from them - their magical life essence. This curse reflects outwards on her odd appearance… one green eye and the other blue, with white streaks dividing her long black hair. Blotches of grey are scattered across her pale skin. She clutches tightly to a scroll at her side. They disappear into the castle, leaving her alone in the dark garden. As it always is, she reaffirms to herself. Kind Aada might not even care to acknowledge her even if she had known she was there, unlike Atgeir, who she is sure saw her. Yet she has another matter to attend to, further outside.

Walking through the palace's lush gardens, making their way to the rear entrance. Atgeir and Aada stroll comfortably in each other's company. They pass a patrolling palace guard adorned in glistening light-plated steel armor, a long hibiscus red coat, and dark halberd in hand. The guard gives a slight bow as they pass, Atgeir responding with but a glance, while Aada expresses a little greeting. She falls slightly behind Atgeir and hastily catches up to his side.

At the rear entrance, they open the heavy dark oak door and head inside. Atgeir pauses… the marbled obsidian-tiled passageway reflects the blueish flames flickering in ornate wall-mounted torches along the walls. He glares at Aada as she stands opposite him. Unexpectedly bluntly, he states: "We're here, Aada! Be on your way then, I must get back to my arcane training for tomorrow's grand event."

She walks away but halts to ask, "Are you going back out on your own….. to work on that ever-so-dangerous spell?"
"What about it…. I am going to master that spell, Aada. It's nothing for you to worry about; I'm confident with that." Atgeir declares with determination, "So yes, after all, the heir to the Severne throne should also be powerful in magic, not just some charismatic leader…. but a powerful one, and that test match will show this to father, that I am going to be that." He says, grinning with a dramatic bow….. stopping before adding another thought. "You will eventually get it when you grow up, still …. that's doubtful."

Aada just stands there, looking confused and a tad annoyed at Atgeir's arrogance and air of superiority: "You could have expressed yourself with much more grace and kindness. I just wanted to know if you needed help or something… You used to always train together with Leifur…. I just thought..." she ends her sentence with greater caution.

"Are you done!" he cuts her short, his voice sharp and bitter, and she steps back, clutching her loose sangria purple shawl.

"Yes….Right…" She says hesitantly.

"Great, just perfect." He grins widely as he exclaims. Glad he is done with this entire conversation.

Aada walks away into the palace, getting in a kind final word: "Just don't get yourself hurt." She says, not being someone to stay mad at anyone, no matter what they say to her.

Annoyed, Atgeir rolled his head at her words; he never got why she was always so overbearingly kind, even when he talked down to her.

Never mind that he has something to get back to, turning around.

He strides away confidently, determined to perfect the volt star spell this time.

Shutting the palace's door quietly behind him, he heads back out at night.

CHAPTER 3
The match is upon us

Eilif stands on the side of the giant Sulfren's carcass, holding onto his injured arm. These were much harder to slay - the beasts increase their strength as they remain alive. Their masters might be gone, yet they fight on persistently, wreaking havoc wherever they go. "Such powerful and resilient.... yet such a pathetic bunch of creatures. Mindlessly attacking anything that moves, their minds..... forever dwelling in the grasp of war, unaware it ended centuries ago." Eilif says under his breath, disgusted by the Sulfren's endless pillage of rage and destruction.

Enveloping his right hand in black flames, Eilif points it at the carcass, shooting the dark fire at it, setting it ablaze. He does the same to the smaller Sulfrens lying slain across the stone floor, ensuring the monsters won't rise back up from the dead. The room fills with smoke, and Eilif exits it with his crows close behind. As they walk through the ancient hall, Nerium moves closer to Larkspur. "Are the Sulfrens usually this tough to defeat ?" She asks him quietly. "No, these monsters are getting stronger, more coordinated….. they are adapting," Larkspur answers in a whisper. "Great…. they are getting stronger, so what? It doesn't matter." She whispers with a sigh, dreading the thought.

Nerium moves away from Larkspur and then walks closer to Nightshade. "Did you hear that certainly? This will spark your interest in learning more about the Sulfren menace ?" Nerium asks him, still keeping her tone down. Nightshade looks over to her with a stoic expression. "No, not at all. It doesn't change anything; we'll just have to fight them as always…. it doesn't matter; we will just have to get stronger to fulfill our duty." He answers bluntly, annoyed by the question. "Right, I should have expected you to say that. You can't just try and look at the bigger picture; figuring this out can prevent so much suffering." Nerium whispers back, quite frustrated with his attitude.

"You should listen to your betters, Nerium. This is not for either of you or myself to solve." Eilif speaks up. Catching her entirely off guard, she thought he couldn't hear them as they were bickering behind him in whispers. "Of course, your Highness." Nerium responds, a bit startled. "Perfect, keep that in mind going forward. Uncovering the Sulfren's sudden growth in strength is up to my greatest scholars to unravel." Eilif stoically states how it should be dealt with. Ambling behind him, with a lowered head: "I understand, your highness." Nerium downheartedly replies to her king's statement. Following him to the frigid outdoors of the outskirts, they have done what they came here to do, and now it's time to head back home. Where Nerium is currently set to figure out what is happening to the sulfrens on her own time, and when her fellow crows and the king aren't aware of what she is doing, can she even piece it all together on herself?

Sitting alone in a dark, damp vine and moss-covered cave, barely visible among swirling mysterious mist, only the bottom half of the magnificent pale, translucent feminine figure, with dark crimson markings crossing her body. Her attention focused intently ahead. Eyes shining with a faint violet glow.

"I can feel it.… it's time for the next phase of the plan.… to commence, my love, the beast is prepared, waiting," She speaks calmly, slowly emphasizing her words, pointing ahead. "Everything is ready. Just have to do one more thing." She slowly closes her outstretched hand. A barely audible voice replies, muffled by the fog. "Perfect, my love." The mysterious fog-veiled figure in the shifting shadows comments with a sickly sweet tone.

The other one is in the cave, obscure in view. Says something; the other's blunt response is inaudible under in the thick waves of fog, endlessly swirling and blending.

A cold, gusty zephyr blows through the azure sky, carrying the prospects of a new day.

The golden morning sun gently glows warm into the bedroom of the thick stone wall of the Hyvits palace. The sleeping Aada senses the early morning sunlight on her fair face, and her long-lashed eyes flutter open as a butterfly flaps its dainty wings. Getting up slowly with her hair a mess on her head. She looks inquisitively down at her hands, wondering what that dream was about, her head dazed. "What was that about ?……..uh.…" Shaking her head slightly. "I think.… no matter, this can wait.… uh." She says, shifting her view to the foot of the bed. Sleeping beside her, her beloved Pet, Ove, brightens Aada's mood instantly. His long grey, furry, weasel-like frame stretched out comically near her feet, on his back. Little paws hanging limp. In peaceful slumber. His fur, with its yellow slips along the length of the almost snake-like slender body, matched the streaks of morning glow across the bed.

"Good morning, Ove. Rise and shine, boy." She says calmly. "What an exciting day. Father is taking on Atgeir in his final test match today! Great, right!" Aada ponders a moment about what Atgeir could be doing, still curious about what he is doing, considering what happened last night, if he was up early, preparing?

Then again, he might just be resting somewhere, unconcerned about it. He is the overconfident type, always sure of his abilities. Still, sometimes that's not a good thing. No matter, those thoughts can wait for now.

"Come on, boy. First, Let's get a bite to eat. We will surely see Atgeir later today at his important match."

Ove rises up promptly, wagging his tail at the mention of food. His little hazel eyes shimmers with glee. Aada gives a soft chuckle at her pet's apparent excitement.

Little beams of light seep through the narrow, slitted windows to warm the dark servant passages of the palace with a yellow glow. Throughout it, scurrying busily along these deep passageways, a group of strange small humanoid creatures silently go about their chores, wearing loose brown and maroon leather attire over their purple rune-engraved opalescent cloudy grey stone body. Each has a shaggy mane of juniper green hair over their rounded heads and glistening gem-like orange eyes. These creatures are known as servsi golems. They are humble beings, solely created to keep the palace clean.

They all hold diligently onto a washcloth, water bucket, feather duster, or a small broom and sack to collect the dust they sweep up.

About two or three of them, breaking away at each exit point, lead each into a different palace room as the servsis continue down the passage to fulfill their cleaning duties. The passageways eventually exit into the palace's grand library.

They spread out as they entered the magnificent sprawling room with its immensely high ceiling and three large stained glass windows adorned with teal, blue, green, and gold hues. Each window displays a mural of a masked elven sorcerer performing different spells: the first shows the sorcerer conjuring fire, ice, and lightning flowing around him, the other shows the sorcerer levitating and facing forward, and the last of a sorcerer holding a glimmering sword in an arc sweep. The sun's light cascaded 'through the multicolored glass onto the dark stone floor. The walls are lined with large bookcases packed with books, tomes, and grimoires. These bookcases stretch all the way to the marble ceiling, ladders, and wooden walkways, making them accessible.

The dutiful servsi scurry about hither and dither, going on with their duties. One little fellow holding a bucket heads further into the library. He sprints carefully but is more focused on the contents of the bucket than on where he is going, trying not to spill water everywhere.

Not noticing what is ahead, the servsi rushes into an indigo velvet sofa. The creature falls flat on its behind with a plop.

Clumsily getting up, he looks up at the impressive frame of Atgeir, sitting regally on the plush sofa. The prince's face shows signs of how tired he is from spending all night trying to master that all-important spell, and annoyed at seeing this clumsy little servsi knocking into his seat. Atgeir glares at the small creature frighteningly.

It jumped back hastily in fright, bolting past the other chairs in the middle of the great library as fast as it could, holding the bucket tight with both hands and disappearing into the far recesses of the room. Atgeir is again left alone to continue, looking through his thoughts as before he was interrupted.

He turned his focus back to what was in front of him: to a dark alder table where a pile of books were stacked, some lying wide open. Pages filled with sketches of strange contraptions, stones, and plants - a myriad of information is contained in these pages on various ways to craft small magical explosive weapons.

His attention is intently drawn to one book on ancient magic, precisely a page with a drawing of a strange red wave emanating from a particular type of gem called pulse Crystals. These can be infused with mana to make a large blast. It does not work consistently, but this could work!

With his countless hours working on mastering the powerful spell that he will have to use in the test against his father, the night-long practice session, the powerful spell he chose to master. An Ultima, as one of these spells, is known as the one that was created and perfected by his great grandfather ages back: the volt star spell…

All wasted.

Nothing to show for the effort. Now Atgeir is scouring for information to find a way to fake it. A last-minute backup plan to succeed. He refuses to fail this test; there is nothing worse than failure in his eyes; he has to get something to fake the spell without his father or the rest of his family spectating his test. If he wins this, he will train under his father and not just some tutor. To learn more potent spells beyond anything that he can be taught by anyone else.

This has to be it.

Plod… plod… plod…

The sound reaches him. Footsteps…… nearby….., it's getting closer; they sound too heavy to be one of the servsis scampering about, but not too heavy. It has to be her; come to check on him before the match. Hastily, Atgeir closes up all the books before him, swiftly hiding them underneath the table, taking another one from behind his back. Sitting with his back straightened, looking with feigned slight interest at the book's pages.

Gracefully strolling in from behind the corner into view, his mother Sia, with her long jet black waist-length hair, laying neatly over her shimmering silvery white gown with light violet floral patterns at the bottom, trailing behind her as she moves towards Atgeir, her calming blue eyes looking upon him. "Good morning, my son. Glad to see you are reading up before your match today." She says warmly." Still, I didn't suspect I would find you here. I thought you would have completed preparing tomorrow." She sits on the seat next to him.

"Morning, Mother." Atgeir returns the greeting politely, holding the book slightly to the side of his face as he looks towards her. Written on the leather cover in artistic bold red strange letters, in their language reading: Different forms of arcane combat techniques. So, she can see what Atgeir is reading up on while not expressing his frustration and hiding his tiredness. "No, I'm done with preparation. I'm just going over a few things, making sure I'm well prepared for the fight for my final test match." Atgeir says confidently, gently placing the closed book on the table.

"Oh, that's good, my son….. great….." she replies, and then looks away into the distance, fidgeting with her intricate moonstone jeweled silver necklace, momentarily lost in thought and memory… she continues to talk, almost forgetting where she is or who she is talking to: "Your brother would have finished his combat tests before you if he was still here with us now… with us here….. I just wonder Leifur would… uh.. where is he….. where could he be…. is he."

Noticing his mother's melancholy stare, gazing away into the distance, Atgeir reaches out to her with a sigh, touching her arm. "Mother, you are doing it again." He shakes her a bit, speaking gently to her.

Sia gave a little gasp of fright, realizing she was drifting off into a world of memory and longing again. She snaps out of it, looking at him again. "oh….. uh….. right. Apologies, I just can't keep my mind from wandering. Where was I…." she says, stumbling through her words. Atgeir shakes his head slightly, concerned. She has not been the same, even ages after Leifur's disappearance, a part of her still believing he might still be alive out there, and another that accepted he was gone. She even taught him how to create crystal constructs from mana to build intricate sculptures. A practice to show how great one is at controlling one's flow and precise use of mana, with his mother being great at it, considering she is proficient with healing magic. Such things his mother loves to do dearly in her spare time, no longer able to keep her mind from drifting away. He just can't understand how this still affects her, even after more than a century of Leifur's sudden disappearance.

Sia notices her son's expression of concern, unmasked upon his face, as he is about to say something to her…

"Oh….. never mind…. Very well, let me not keep you any further. I'm sure you want a few moments to prepare your mind for the battle ahead. I shall see you later then…. Geir," She kindly says as she gets up from her chair, slowly walks past him with a weak smile, and continues out of the room.

Atgeir watches her as she leaves until she is out of sight around a corner. He hurriedly looks around the room, seeing if anyone is nearby.

It's clear.

Leaning down, he retrieves the book on the pulse crystal from underneath the table with a wide grin gleaming on his sly face.

He will just have to a pulse crystal, and fortunately, he knows someone who can provide him with such an exquisite item at short notice. This might be considered wrong, using it to succeed in this test instead of an ultima spell he mastered beforehand, but it does not matter; the outcome is all that matters. Besides, he will have lots of time afterward to get skilled in it. He is sure this will all work out well.

Now, he is confident he is ready.

Sia walks out to a large terrace at the back of the palace. It is a tranquil area, paved with a white quartzite and obsidian floor, with a stained glass canopy of blues, purples, and teal covering the terrace, and underneath five black steel tables with Aada sitting at one. She sits on the opposite side of the table from her daughter, who has a bowl filled with a custard-like porridge made of sweet purple fruit with some powder sprinkled over it and refined crushed grains and mint, called a petrella dish, along with a cup of tea. Aada is focused, throwing a treat from a small ornate chest on the table to an eager Ove, standing beside her on the floor, wagging his tail in delight as he catches a treat, devouring it in no time.

Sia notices one of the little Golems scurrying by. "Servsi, hurry on over here." She calls it to her. The servsi hurries over to the table, kneeling down next to Sia. "Go get me a slice of palevioletred petal cake and a cup of tea." She orders the Golem.

The Servsi gets up and immediately takes off, dashing through a small door, one made for these golems to traverse into and throughout the palace in order to fetch what she asked for from the palace's cook. servsis helps clean and retrieve things, but not for anything more complicated, such as cooking a meal. These kinds of Golems aren't bright yet efficient in their basic tasks. "Today's going to be exciting, I'm quite curious how such a match is even done." Aada says, getting her mother's attention. "It's more of a showcase of one's use and mastery of a spell than about actually winning," Sia answers her, aware Atgeir wouldn't be capable of defeating Eilif in a fight as he currently is. "That will make his odds better in succeeding at it…." Aada pauses abruptly as she thinks she said something rude about Atgeir. Not that he wouldn't have any chance to win in a fight with father…. Atgeir puts in a lot of work at becoming stronger at arcane combat, so I guess….. then again…. I mean…." Aada tries to say something about how he would stand a chance. "Calm down. You haven't said anything wrong." Sia warmly reassures her daughter in a soothing tone.

Aada smiles back, relieved she wasn't being mean. "You are such… such a kind soul, my dear. I'm certain you will make a magnificent healer. When your test comes to advance your training, Aada, you certainly will succeed." Sia says proudly. Thinking back on all the progress she has achieved in learning arcane healing. "Thanks, mother. That's a very nice thing of you to say." Aada cheerfully expresses her appreciation as Ove leaps onto her head. Sia holds her hand over her mouth, giggling at the critter with its tiny front paws dangling over Aada's face. "I think you should place Ove back on the floor. He does tend to shed; better not have him that close to the food." Sia suggests as she regains her composure, pointing at her pet, lounging comfortably across Aada's head. "Right….. sorry, I'll do just that." She says, hastily proceeding to do what her mother told her. Gently plopping down Ove next to her on the stone floor. Patting the little creature on his fluffy head, she gives him another treat, which he devours again.

Aada smiles happily at him, glad her pet enjoys it. "He's such a ravenous little Auqine." Sia joyously expresses her affection for Ove, rolling onto his back with a cheeky look on his fuzzy face. "He is the most adorable critter there is." Aada happily adds.

Sia giggles at her daughter's love and enthusiasm towards her pet, getting Aada to laugh. Going merrily about this pleasant morning, talking to each other outside on the terrace.

CHAPTER 4
The proving match

Exhausted but victorious, the warriors stride, throwing open the large oak door. A bit disorientated by being teleported back by Larkspur's spell. Still, they appear composed and dignified, not showing any signs of tiredness.

They stride down the corridor, King Eilif, with his Crows following after him, returned from their successful slaying of the group of sulfrens in the ruined temple. The battle was fierce, yet they only sustained minor injuries and damages, a few cuts and scrapes. He dare not rest yet; he has one more thing to do today, and he's made it back in time to do it. "Wolfsbane, head to the archive and report to Vilho Rula on today's sulfren extermination so he can add it to the records of encounters. Nightshade, Larkspur, Nerium, there is no further need for you now; you're all dismissed!" Eilif commands the Crows, keeping a steady pace forward.

Wolfsbane falls back swiftly as commanded, heading out to complete his task, while the others slowly dismiss in various directions. They leave King Eilif to make his way to the palace's arena. His footsteps echo through the marble passageway. He is going off to test his son one final time. He must know if he has sufficiently mastered the combat aspect of magic.

He expects his son to excel in the test, and nothing less will suffice. The boy did quite well in the previous fights with his combat trainer, yet…. the time to prove himself was at hand!

Standing in the hallway next to the door leading into the arena outside. Atgeir looks down at the small red crystal held tightly in his dark, gloved hand. Obtained quickly by his contact, an adventurous sort of fellow who could get anything you requested for a price. This is going to bring him victory, surely!

He carefully places it in his coat pocket, out of sight. He looks down and picks up his silver-clawed gauntlets on the ground beside him. Putting them on over his gloves while a devious grin spreads over his sharp features.

Facing ahead, he pushes the door open.

Leaning quietly against the wall, she sketches in a dark blue floral patterned leather book. In the back row of decorative dark oak benches, with sculpted obsidian and alabaster detailed frames attached to each end, Thyra looks up from her drawing, watching intently from her shadowed vantage point. She sees her mother and younger sister, with her pet, sleeping wrapped around her shoulders. They take their seats some distance away in front of her, looking over the marble wall separating the spacious arena and the elevated rows of seating to the one side of this massive hall in the palace.

Atgeir's private arcane combat tutor, a rigid and disciplined instructor known as Cuyler the Austere, sits above them on the higher-up rows. He must have come to see if his student would be victorious in this test. If Atgeir fails, it will reflect poorly on his abilities to teach. Especially since this student is the son of their King.

Her eyes wander further up the rows to spot her aunt Eir Solstris seated; she did show up for Atgeir's match. Still, she was the only one who had the time, considering that their extended family holds high positions in the realm, and it had been busier than usual these past couple of days, even outside the capital.

Although she does not believe Atgeir even deserves anyone to show up to watch him fight his little test match. Out of everyone in her family, she considers him to be the worst of them all. Atgeir is just a conniving, manipulative scoundrel, and it sometimes feels like she is the only one who realizes it. She ponders, continuing to draw a strange shimmering, long, split-tailed regal bird known as a Zelene crane. Adding a couple more touches, she knows that she always has had a love and fascination with birds. The beauty and grace shown by most of them captivate her. Especially this bird that is so revered and adored by so many, unlike herself, that is.

Looking back again as she hears a door open, she spots Atgeir swaggering into the arena, his head held high, a smug expression on his face, and on the other side, King Eilif's standing resolute, her imposing father. Standing alongside him is an unusually short elderly elf clad in a long white and teal robe, his head adorned by a long-tailed hood.

Thyra closes her book, giving a frustrated sigh. Looks like it's about to start. Hopefully, this will be entertaining, at the very least. She looks on at it begrudgingly.

"Today shall be the day of Prince Atgeir's final test to prove his skill in arcane combat against his father, the revered King Eilif. They will contest in his chosen class of magic of the elemental nature, the electromancy branch. He must use at least three advanced spells and an Ultima to pass!" Standing between the two elven royals, the elderly-robed elf announced to the spectators. He is the match supervisor, making sure to spot Atgeir if he tries to cheat or use any hidden or underhanded tactics during the fight.

The massive hall is hushed. Silent with expectation. Everyone waits excitedly.

The silence is suddenly shattered by two trumpeters who step out of the shadows and blast a ceremonious fanfare, announcing the start of this crucial final test mast!

When the trumpeters stop, two drummers step forward and begin to pulse out a steady and exhilarating drum beat. Expectancy rises!

The supervisor, now standing far to the side, shouts out. "Commence the match!" He lifts his arm in the air.

Immediately, the King and his young opponent spring to action! They take an alert stance, maintaining focused, direct eye contact. King Eilif steadily moves to the left... Atgeir mirrors his movement. The two combatants pace like two fighting wolves, sizing each other up, poised and wound up to attack, monitoring each other minutely, waiting for the first one to attack.

Atgeir, somewhat impatient by nature, and ever over-confident, makes the first move:

He starts in a slow walk to the side, developing into a jog, and his body becomes enveloped in crimson electricity as he goes to a sprint. He appears like a speeding ball of lightning basting out in an arch, directed towards Eilif's side.

Breaking out of it in mid-air, he executes an electrified roundhouse kick.

Eilif reacts, bringing up his hand and blocking it with a small light shield.

Atgeir falls back to the ground with a backflip, hastily to avoid his father's counterattack, landing a few meters away from Eilif with a slight thud.

Atgeir assumes a low fighting stance while King Eilif saunters toward him. "A thunder comet followed by a lightning talon kick, impressive. Still, let's see how you will counter this then." Eilif exclaims, forming a blade of translucent golden mana over his hand. Holding it close to his chest, ready to strike, he lunges forward, kicking the ground behind him into a massive cloud of dust, slashing upwards at the prince.

Atgeir ducks, avoiding the hit, but just barely. Rolling away to the side, he stumbles back up, only to notice a projectile whizzing towards him at high speed, one of Eilif's dark flaming Chakrams. Reflexively, he enhances his gauntlets with mana, blocking the attack. He pushes it away with his entire strength, sending it careering off. "Don't hold back… or are you going easy on me, Father?" Atgeir says smugly while staggering back, and then he electrifies the clawed tips of his gauntlet in a deep crimson voltage. Slashing forward creates waves of scarlet shimmering force shooting towards his opponent!

The King launches upwards, avoiding the attack, levitating above the arena's floor. "Not at all, my son. But I thought with that lightning ribbons spell, I had better step up my game then." Eilif responds sarcastically.

Eilif redirects his Chakrams, flying above them, swirling above them in black flames, at Atgeir.

Eilif's counterattack begins. In a high-speed fury of flying blades, Atgeir dodges and weaves between them to escape the impact. Jabbing each one from the air with his mana-enhanced gauntlet between each opening he sees.

Atgeir looks up with determination in his eyes…. it is time. He got it right to grab the pulse crystal while he was dodging.

He bolts away from Eilif, holding his hands close to each other, creating a ball of scarlet electricity, the pulse crystal hidden between his fingers. Pretending that he is about to do the Volt Star spell. Time to blow him away with this one, Atgeir thinks to himself cockily.

Halting in his tracks, pulling back his hand, ready to pour some of his mana into it, and set it flying for a massive explosion.

Three……. two……. one….. what?

He can't move his arm, it's… it's…. restraint….

"Did you really think you would get that past my old eyes, my prince?" He hears the supervisor's voice. Atgeir's body freezes in terror at this revelation; he has been caught out! Looking behind him, the old elf stands holding his arm back. The supervisor snatches the crystal from Atgeir's hand, holds it, and presents it to his king.

Eilif levitates beside them, taking it from the supervisor's hand. Looking at it closely in his palm.

His eyes glaring at his son: "Come with me…. now!" He says coldly, gesturing the way.

Eilif walks away with Atgeir, who is filled with dread. The supervisor watches him pass by while shaking his head in disappointment.

Sitting nervously in the spectator's rows, Aada watches as they leave the arena. Ove is sleeping around her shoulders, unaware of what transpired. "Do you think Father will go hard on Atgeir? He did just break the rules of this important test match?" She asks her mother while gently stroking Ove's head.

"There's nothing to be concerned about. I'm confident your father will be fair, and Atgeir's punishment won't be that horrible."

Laughter breaks out from behind her. Stunned, they turned to see Eir holding her sides in laughter. "Really, like he would go easy on anyone, especially regarding family!" She says, wiping a tear from her dark grey eyes.

"That's an incredibly rude to say; what do you even mean by that?" Aada says with a brow raised. Eir regains her composure, flattening down her unruly, wavy blonde hair, smirking. Placing her arm on her lap, leaning forward, she says in a hushed voice: "One thing I'll tell you, you don't know what he does when someone really messes up, especially if it's someone from close to him. He's going to make sure Atgeir won't forget this. Getting things perfect and back to how he wants it to be. That's just how he is, his entire life." She says cockily, pointing down to her.

Aada responds meekly. "That's not right. My father won't do that; he's not like that…." Eir just laughs at her obliviousness. "Really, I know your father far more than you do…. I have witnessed what he can do." She points out to her niece.

So Aada replies back, and then she does, and it goes on and on with Thyra leaning against the wall, uninterested, watching them arguing.

Thyra stands back up as their heated conversation continues, not one of them noticing as she just walks out of the arena. Thyra has something more important that she must attend to now. Their squabbling does not interest her at the least.

Facing Atgeir in the dark hall, with the supervisor standing respectfully from them, Eilif begins: "Atgeir… how could you have done that… to even think you would try such a thing." He says, holding the crystal up towards him.

Eilif crushes it to red dust, glaring angrily at Atgeir. He is released from the old elf's grasp. "Pathetic! Cheating on your test. Especially with a pulse crystal, the most unreliable gem. They barely work at the best of times. Your brother would never have done this, especially before so many eyes!" Furious at his son, he throws the crystal dust into the air. Atgeir tries to defend himself, to weasel himself out of this most uncomfortable situation, but he just can't. He is restrained by his deep respect and real fear for his father. He dare not form even a single word. He listens as the King continues… "This is a test of skill, not this…. you disappoint me! I can't keep being lenient on your actions, so…. as punishment, I am sending you to the outskirts. You will assist at the grueling abyss defense tower for five years. Learning some real discipline!"

Not thinking about it, Atgeir snaps out. "You can't just send me to that place...." He stops, regretting his words and seeing his father's cold wrath increase.

"Did I say five? I meant eight. Do you have anything else to say about it?" He asks Atgeir scornfully.

Atgeir nods weakly.

"Great! You will be sent away promptly tomorrow. You will be taught how a Solstris is supposed to conduct themself." Eilif strides off, leaving Atgeir alone, thinking about what will happen. He also ponders about his brother and that his father made him remember with his biting remark that he was still in the great Leifur's shadow, even now.

CHAPTER 5
Shining opportunity

Dashing down the dark hallway. Thyra stops as she hears someone slowly approaching.

She peaks out from behind a corner, waiting. Holding onto a neatly folded piece of paper. She sees Atgeir coming closer, appearing miserable and defeated, a state she never thought she would see him in. The one she despises the most, but now that does not matter. She has come to ask him something of great importance, and he is now motivated to help her.

She comes out into his view, blocking his path. "Apologies, brother. Can I have a moment of your time?" She says with false concern. Atgeir just tries to walk past her. She hastily walks before him, blocking him as he tries again to escape. Atgeir is trying to get past while still keeping his distance

from her. "I won't let you pass till you hear me out." She says with
determination as she keeps up the blockade.

Giving a heavy sigh, crossing his arms, he concedes.

"Fine… what do you have to say? Just make it quick, then. I'm not really in
the mood for this." He finally snaps at her out of pure frustration. It's the
first time he has spoken to her in ages.

Holding out the paper, she says calmly. "Read this, I found this on a table in
our father's study, unopened. I think you will be interested in it." He grabs it
from her hand, unfolding it. Reading it silently.

Your Majesty, this is a message of great importance.

*The Thiar realms have found a way to send a telepathic warning that a
great beast of immense power has appeared in the Thiar realm. Leaving
death and havoc in its path. It is being called the Blood Chimera. We
believe in time; if it is not stopped and the warriors of that realm cannot
slay it themselves, it will find a way to break out of the realm, free to start
invading other known realms, including ours.*

*From descriptions I have gathered, it is a bipedal beast with antlers of a
stag on top, a dark mane, the legs of a wolf, most of its body covered in red
scales, including its arms with its hands adorned with long sharp claws and
wings similar to a bat, a long whip-like tail with a spiked bony club at its
end and the face of a man.*
*It has scorched the realm with its strength of fire and lightning, along with
its army of grotesque beasts it has created.*

I propose sending a team to dispose of the beast before it is too late.

"This could be a way to get back into father's good graces, don't you think? To become the hero that stopped this formidable monster. You will be remembered in the future, for centuries, when you are crowned as the King who stopped a deadly threat to the known realms." Thyra injects her idea into his mind enthusiastically.

Atgeir's eyes light up, and a slight smirk appears, but it disappears quickly. "Wait…. why don't you go and do this yourself, to get some recognition? You surely would want that. I can tell you don't like me." He questions her suspiciously, waving the piece of paper at her.

"Yes, I hate you and…. getting admiration and recognition for slaying it would be great, but I would rather not have all this end in disaster if I failed. Besides, did you forget I can't use magic? I can't take on that beast." She looks down submissively. "This could also lead to a favor from you." She concludes.

"I guessed that much….. what favor do you want exactly? No one does anything for nothing."

"Just want you to help me catch a Zelene crane when you return. I want to keep one close to me…. sort of like a beautiful pet. That sounds like a suitable trade; you gain fame and recognition for the ages, while I gain a gorgeous bird that will be all mine forever and ever."

"That sounds…. reasonable… you have a deal. Just one thing: how will I get to the Thiar realm in the first place. All the realm gates leading out have been destroyed?"

Thyra nods and answers readily. "I have planned this far in advance until I realized my complete lack of any arcane abilities, making this dangerous for me, so I didn't go ahead, but this preparation will help you now. One secret realm gate is left, hidden in the Kartez mountain range."

Grinning widely, he says, "Good! Still, I will have to prepare for this journey. You just need to give me some directions to this portal and how to activate it."

"Right, I shall make you a map of it and then leave it for you somewhere in your room." She agrees, nodding enthusiastically. Glad he has decided on her proposal.

She hesitantly starts to walk away from him.

Atgeir shouts out to her: "One more thing, what were you doing skulking last night, hiding behind the foliage?" She looks around, surprised. "Just wanted to go somewhere calm and open to draw some beautiful night scenery. It helps clear my head; I promise no one outside the palace even saw me."

"Why do I even ask. I should have known if you were doing something, it would be something so dull. I won't tell you, though, if you don't mess with me, right Thyra." He glares at her before walking away, hearing her giving an uninterested reply. "Rest assured, I won't. I know who you are." Her departing words are just a whisper, so he can't hear them: "Just some selfish conniving rat."

The sun crosses the sky, setting away off in the distance. Its sinking below the horizon brings to life the starry darkness of the night.

Busy in his room, Atgeir hastily packs items in a small light grey backpack. A couple of items are needed for his journey: a sharp dagger, a purple cloak, and a pouch full of pure radiance crystals to sell for the Thiar realm's currency so he can buy anything else he needs there.

Closing it up, he swings it over his back, strapping it on tightly.

Prepared and wearing an imperial purple coat embroidered with his family coat of arms in silver on the shoulders - a shield with rays of sunlight beaming from the top, leafed branches winding from the bottom to the sides, and on top a falcon soaring upward, wings like a crescent moon, with two crossed spears behind it. A ring of diamonds hover above its head.

He is equipped with silver gauntlets and dark dray boots adorned with silver greaves.

Leaving behind a note not explaining where he went but that he would be gone for a while, and when he returns, they would be proud of what he had accomplished and remembered for it for millennia long come.

Moving silently out of his room, heading into a dark hallway, holding out his hand, he creates a small crimson ball of light to see ahead far clearer.

He creeps along, illuminating numerous paintings on the white wall as he passes, some portraying his great ancestors whom he aspires to, while others showing scenes from the divine war: elven soldiers fighting against these gigantic radiating beings with their hideous-looking white-scaled beasts. Yet others portray beautiful forest landscapes, one of them a herd of white deer next to a serene lake or a falcon soaring over a snowy field.

As he walks by, one of the paintings catches his attention: painted a hundred and ten years ago when he was just a child. It displays his family, excluding Thyra. When Leifur was still with them. His brother standing next to him in the portrait. His jet-black hair was neatly combed, and his gray eyes dully stared into nothingness as if he wished to be elsewhere. Leifur could get it right by standing in one place for a long time. Atgeir chuckles at the thought.

Thinking that his big brother would never see how far he had come and how far he would go. What a shame, but because he was gone now. Atgeir was now the crown prince, closer to going to greater heights than where he is now. Nonetheless, there is a deep sadness within him for it. He cared for and respected his brother deeply. Indeed, it is a complicated feeling.

There was no time for such thoughts.

Stepping away, he presses on towards a window at the end of the hallway.

He leaps onto it and climbs out of it, down to the ground below.

Blue fire burns brightly over a pile of crystal in an exquisitely sculpted marble fireplace and sits around an obsidian and alabaster table. Right in front of it are both Eilif and Sia. A set of intricate violet-colored glass tea cups and a teapot is on the table before them, filled with tea made from the leaves, a special type of sweet plant only found in the Severne realm, known as a sinzro vine.

"Can't you reconsider Atgeir's punishment, Eil. There surely is a better way to get your point across to him in another way…. a kinder way." Sia says politely.

"My decision is final, my dear. There is nothing you can say that can change my mind. The boy has to be disciplined. For being born a Solstris, he has to stand as an example to the people, to be looked up to." He declares it resolutely. Picking up a cup, he takes a careful sip.

"I understand holding up appearances, yet I still don't agree with sending him to that dreadful place. It is known for the most sulfren sightings. What is more, other vicious beasts are prowling those scorched as well, lifeless parts, and the air there is suffocating. It is just that…." Sia says, ending her sentence abruptly, looking up. Her mind started to drift off again... staring at the ceiling for a while before snapping out of it and seeing Eilif watching her with an unyielding look on his face…. so she decided to just…. give up on trying to change his mind, realizing he won't let go of his decision. "Never mind….. I just hope Atgeir can handle it out there." She looks own. Eilif walks over to her and bends down to put his hand on her shoulder. "It will be horrible, grueling, and even painful there, yet I am sure he will return better than when he went there. I know for sure our son is someone who will never give up that easily; he always finds a way."

Sia looks up at him, a hesitant smile forming, feeling more hopeful than before.

Atgeir runs swiftly between the gigantic Spruce trees of the Valkorn Forest. The moon's light made his path visible. Following the map Thyra made for him and something else needed for later, he found hidden underneath a pile of books on his desk.

Sprinting around large jagged boulders, vaulting over fallen trees, and even leaping across a wide gorge, he finally makes it to an upward slope, dashing upwards over it.

He comes to a sudden halt as he looks at the sight ahead of him: the Kartez mountain range in the distance. Far away from the clifftop he is standing on.

Jumping down, he enchants his body with mana to survive the long fall.

He hits the ground below with a hard crash. The impact sends dirt and dust flying everywhere! Then the prince bursts out of the dust billow, running off towards the maintain. The portal is located towards the cave, as shown by the map.

CHAPTER 6
Heading out to the Thiar realm

The sounds of water droplets seeping through the cracks of the cave ceiling, hitting the rough stone cave floor, echoing through the large cavernous chamber. Each solid stone wall is covered with various regular and glowing kinds of moss covered in strange purple berries.

In the center rise two large jade pillars reaching up to the cave's ceiling, engraved with strange red markings - vines and moss grown across it with a round jade podium with similar markings in front of it.

The prince strides into the chamber, heading straight towards the structure: the realm gate. He takes out of his pocket a strange white disk with the symbol of a hawk on it - a traveler's stone. He places the stone on top of the podiums in a hole that it fits into perfectly. The symbols on all the structures light up with a deep crimson glow, forming a swirling reddish purple portal, as tiny wisps of light drift gently around it, fading in and out through the air.

Picking the disk back up, he puts it back into his coat pocket, hesitantly walking toward the glowing portal ahead and stepping into it. A strange sensation washes over his body, and his vision blurs in a cascade of colors and strange whirring sound around him…. then….

As the vortex of colors drifts away, Atgeir is met with an astonishing sight. The vast stretch of a strange star-filled sky with massive floating dark rocks, made of the same kind of stone as the large platform he is standing on, with a peculiar golden ocean surrounding it, all within the swirling purplish blue and red dark void, hundreds of suns are visible as stars in the far-off darkness, each belonging to a different set of realms. His realms moon orbiting high above him and behind him, in a jade arch with a pedestal in front of it, is a gate similar to the one he had just gone through, containing a colossal, levitating, ethereal black sphere larger than the largest mountain. Upon this large sphere is a large glowing blue sigil of a circle attached to an upward arrow with two sharp angular wings on each side. Radiating from the bottom are four vertical lines.

Suddenly, its portal vanishes. It appears to not stay open forever, only remaining open a few moments after the disk is removed, a fact Atgeir will keep in the back of his head.

Scanning the area, a flock of giant greenish-blue falcons as big as a large oak, each with a saddle strapped on their backs, rest on large steel perches. This must be how to travel from realm to realm; it was so long that Atgeir barely remembered that. How could he have forgotten that much, he wonders.

Atgeir runs towards the flock and picks one with the name Daltido written on the side of its saddle. Climbing on top of it, he sits down, unsure what to do next. He has not read up on realm travel much, and it has been so long since he even traveled to another realm when that was still allowed. When his family sometimes went to any of the other known realms to talk with the royalty of that kingdom, there would be inter-realm meetings at certain times, about a hundred and twelve years ago. He could only faintly remember the world between realms.

As he searches for a way to steer this bird to where he specifically wants to go, he sees a circular opening on the neck near the collar. He carefully inserts his hand into the opening. Lighting up, words form on the collar in his language: speak your destination!

He yells out clearly. "Thiar realm." A glowing green sigil appears on the collar of a downward triangle with an arrow going through it that's pointing left with three large flowers going in an arc around it in a spiral and three horizontal lines going on the right side. As it shows up, the bird's large wings spread open as those words exit his mouth. Taking off at an incredible speed, it flies off over the golden sea. Leaning back in the saddle, he admires the strange scenery. He thinks about what he will do when he arrives there. Maybe pay some fools to help him find this Blood Chimera and slay it.

This will be his moment: the hour to define himself as the powerful future leader of his realm and to get his father to acknowledge the greatness that he feels he deserves, especially since they are so scared the beast finds a way to travel between the known realms without the use of realm gates. That potential indeed makes it a tremendously strong beast to be greatly feared. Still, it surely can't be stronger than him…. he is a descendant of a great and powerful lineage…. can he… no it can't…. what a silly thought that it could happen…....

These ideas race through his head as he rests on the falcon's back, flying right towards his objective at high speeds.

As the swirl of purple fog moves around the dark cave, the translucent feminine figure sits in a hole in the wall, covered half in hanging vines. The woman's figure is obscured by the mist. A slight glow from her eyes shines through the vegetation.

"Things are finally setting right into motion, beautiful, isn't it?" she says, reaching out of the vines and fog, swishing it from side to side. "This beast is a masterful creation; it won't disappoint me. I can feel it, to my core." The figure says, giving a mischievous giggle. A voice from somewhere in front of her responds hesitantly, an incomprehensible and muffled voice.

The figure swats at the fog, dispersing it slightly. "There is nothing to fret about, my love. You will see, soon we will both get what we always dreamed of and get what is owed to us all."

Things go completely dark as the glowing mists slowly dissipate in the caved environment.

Rising from her bed in a daze, Aada's eyes dart around the room. Seeing only the darkness of night, she stares ahead, uncertain of what she witnessed in her sleep.

Why does she keep getting that same dream? What is it trying to show her? She walks towards her room's balcony, opening the large black and white doors and going through a wall of delicate violet shimmering silk curtains with a beautiful frosted pattern hanging in her path. She goes out to get some fresh air to clear her head.

Greeted by a cold, gusty wind, she shudders. She directs her gaze up towards the sky, dotted with stars.

Her little pet Ove leaps onto the balcony railing beside her, startling her a little. "Hi, Ove…. sorry to wake you up, I didn't mean to… You should get back to sleep; it's quite late." Aada quietly says, petting his fuzzy head and getting a friendly chirp from her small friend. Ove lovingly rubs against her arm with his long body before swiftly leaping down to the floor and running back into Aada's room.

Setting her gaze down to him, giving him a gentle pat on his head, she turns her gaze back to the sky…. thinking about what to do?

This is just too strange; what could this even mean? She wants to talk to someone about this, but it is better not to tell anyone for now. At least until she figures out if this is more than just an odd dream, she reasons with herself. No need to get anyone worried for nothing.

CHAPTER 7
Making a beneficial offer

In the far-off Thiar realm, on a calm, clear day. Crouched over in a lush green meadow surrounded by a forest, Kaylan goes meticulously through a pile of bizarre clutter from a large satchel, along with a smooth sphere made of purple lepidolite called the Mind Orb. His long, fluffy rabbit ears perked up with excitement above his white, wild, short hair, with his amber eyes gleaming in his pale face.

Sorting the jumble, he pulls out a strange-shaped crystal dagger and places it on his left. He also retrieves a couple of vials and a deep cobalt-coloured hooked claw.

Turning towards the things he took out, he picks up the dagger with one hand and the claw with the other. He carefully shaves some bits off from the claw into an empty vial with the dagger. Putting the dagger down, he picks up a vial filled with a teal liquid and pours it into the vial with the claw fur shavings. Then he shakes it a bit. It turns a bright crimson red with glowing blue specks floating within.

His face lights up at this color change…. then this enthusiasm suddenly vanishes….. as he senses something large behind him.

His face now expresses pure terror as he sees the space around him turn dark. A foul, rotten gust blows against his back, sending a shiver down his spine and making the bushy tip on his long tail stand on end. Staring back, his gaze is met by a fearsome sight.

It is an ashy reptilian-like head with a row of mangy green fur running down its head, five large blood-red eyes, and rows of yellow dagger-like teeth. Attached to a long serpent body with two arms stretched out at him, armed with long bony blades instead of a hand or a paw, a Terror beast!

Seeing its head lurching back as if to attack, Kaylan leaps instinctively out of its path, the sphere flying off behind him, surrounded by a glow. Stumbling clumsily on the ground away from it, debris falls caused by the beast hitting the hard rocky ground as it tries to bite into him.

Hurriedly, getting up and stumbles forward into a run, the sphere flying off next to him, always following behind him everywhere he goes. The beast behind him shakes the clump of dirt bitten out of its mouth. Slithering fast behind him, the reptilian monster emits a haunting shriek.

As Kaylan runs, he looks back quickly past the hulking beast to the remnants of his precious research, broken and flung everywhere on the ground. Looking back ahead with a sad, pained expression, he escapes into the forest. Kaylan has to make a plan because of his lack of strength at Arcane combat, even though he's studied and practiced it extensively; this thought goes through his head while desperately dodging the beast's every lunge and swipe at him with its bladed arms, transforming in a puff of smoke into a white hare and back again to duck quickly under swipes. He counters the beast by hitting back by sending his sphere to bombard the creature's head repeatedly while he flees. The beast barely even notices Kaylan's feeble attacks, which hardly damage its rugged hide.

Running as fast as he can, he bolts into the forest, leaping through two trees standing beside each other. The beast's head bursts in after him between the two trees, nipping into him but just about ripping off a part of his scarf and leaving a ragged, bleeding cut down his back. Kaylan tumbles onto the ground in a painful landing. He looks up, seeing its head stuck between the tree trunks and the piece of navy blue and maroon scarf fabric tucked between its vicious teeth.

Backing up slowly with the sphere floating beside him, carefully observing the beast. Trying to think of a way to take this monster - surely the creature won't be clever enough to….. it seems to be just a mindless…..

The sound of wood breaking, a crack, and the trees hitting the ground, he turns around, his eyes wide with fright. He dashes away as he sees the beast has freed its head, exploding towards him with vertical scars across its neck. It just sliced through the trees without considering if it would hurt itself. This thing might still be not clever, but it was scarily determined to kill him.

Kaylan frantically sprints deeper into the forest, not seeing much before him. He stumbles down a decline and rolls down, hitting against rocks and protruding roots.

He collides with a hard surface, stopping him suddenly.

…..Kaylan struggles up, his hand holding onto his bruised side, his tunic now torn in various places. Behind him is a strange, ruined jade arch.

His gaze gets drawn up to the beast crashing down towards him. His head races with any strategies to overcome this foe, to use his surroundings to slay it, anything……

Then……

…..a swishing whirling sound erupts behind him with an enveloping glow….

…a violent burst of crimson flares out from it, and a giant ball of lightning shoots out behind him…… electricity.

Launching straight past the beast…. landing…. showing a figure slowly emerging from the voltage….

Silence hangs in the air….. as the beast collapses right in front of his eyes! Its chest bursting open in a gush of purple blood….. its many eyes going a pale deathly white…. what just happened?

Staring at the grotesque beast's hulking form lying collapsed before him, he is repulsed by it, an overwhelming stench of rotten flesh and vegetation emanating from it.

What was this thing even doing here? As if it was waiting for him to come out of that portal. He is about to walk out of it when he is welcomed to the realm by this hideous creature striking at him.

This thing does not match the description of the monster he came to slay. It would be better to burn this monstrosity to cinders and eliminate it. Scarlet electricity forms around his gauntlet. Atgeir points it towards the monster.

"No, stop! That's valuable research material!" Kaylan shouts out, shakily getting up with his little strength, holding onto his fluorite ball and floating him up to his feet. He rushes weakly to stand in front of the carcass, holding his hands out in defense, trembling a bit at the towering Atgeir looming over him as he stands there with his electric spell still aimed at the beast behind him. Atgeir looks down at Kaylan, a strange creature he immediately sees as inferior. "What did you just say, creature? Pick your words wisely, for you speak to prince Atgeir Solstris of the Severne realm." Atgeir says threateningly, coldly.

Kaylan gives a frightened yelp and quickly provides an explanation: "The thing is, I need to get samples to test to figure out what they are and how to get rid of this terrible threat, as they just appeared recently, causing great death and destruction…. and we don't know where these terror beasts came from…. still I am sure this is new to you…." he rambles on, trying to get Atgeir to not destroy the beast's corpse. "You are not from here… or even from this realm... so I shouldn't have thought you would know." he finishes with a nervous smile.

"So you're saying, creature… that you are currently looking into this? I think I might have use for you, after all. Are you alone in this effort, or are you part of some sort of team?" He asks, and Kaylan responds immediately. "Yes, I am assigned to a specialized group formed to go to the forefront to stop this menace; we are called the Arcana regiment. We have gotten far in finding a way to defeat this enemy."

Atgeir gives him a smirk; lowering his hand, he shuts off the crimson electricity on the gauntlet. "This is definitely fate then, that we met. I have a proposition for your creature. You and your Arcana regiment help me find a specific monster, the Blood Chimera, I don't know why you haven't heard of it. The cause for all this world's recent strife, not only will this save your realm, but I will also reward you richly. You can be a guide of sorts with your little squad as backup," Atgeir says, sure to procure some support, especially as he does not know this realm well and there is not much time to spend searching. To make his quest to slay the Blood Chimera faster and easier, he needs help.

Kaylan hastily thinks it over; how does he know this, and why does he think Kaylan knows of it? He must have gotten false information on the matter; he can ask him back at the base for further details. Still, this could be good; they could aid each other. He does not care much for the wealth he might gain for helping, but things are drastic, and one must take whatever help one can get. And he seemed to be quite strong and is confident he knows what is causing this. Filled with hope, Kaylan responds confidently. "You have a deal then." Holding his hand out to shake it, Atgeir just walks past him, ignoring his gesture. "Perfect, then will you take me to the rest of my team? They'll be glad to see you… maybe…. hopefully."

Kaylan puts down his hand, a bit disappointed. "Sure, just let me quickly get a sample from the fallen beast," he says, gesturing back to the terror beast's body.

"Fine…. Just make it quick, then, creature. I really don't have time for anything." Atgeir impatiently tells him.

Kaylan nods down next to the beast, holding onto one of its jagged teeth. He pulls out a knife, jabbing it in between the teeth to pry one out. "By the way, my name is Kaylan; I hope this arrangement works well for both of us." The tooth falls out of the beast's maw. He catches it before it hits the ground.

"Sure, especially for me." Atgeir says, snickering at the thought of it.

Kaylan looks at him, confused by the statement. He gets up. He uses the remnant of his scarf to carry the jagged tooth, tying it onto his belt.

Kaylan then heads off to lead the way to his group's base of operation, bringing back a new ally.

Away in another dense, faraway forest, the chimera sits underneath a tree, its crimson wings spread out. Many small terror beasts roamed around it, skulking around the ground and crawling along the tree lines, bringing back dead animal parts, plants, and dirt.

Adding pieces from the deceased beasts to a towering pile imbues it with dark energy. The mass shapes in front of the chimera into a giant grey salamander-like beast with patches of mangy green fur and long dagger-like metal claws. The chimera smiles at its new creation, basking in it as it runs off to another location to kill and ravage. Interrupted as a pair of flying terror beasts drops the arm of the beast with the bladed arms. Looking down on it, picking it up curiously.

Smelling it, the chimera burst into a pained, twisted laughter. "Another one of them….. come to stop me….. interesting….. It's with one of… those….. who did she send me…… I better see what this one is made of, then….. It's almost time….. for part two." The chimera says in a raspy, broken voice, as black smoke and green fire emanate from its wicked smile.

CHAPTER 8
A very rocky start

Settled proudly on a cliff top over a small village below called Gorseton.
Rests the mighty Fort Borage, a large building erected sturdily out of a
greyish-red stone.

Resting on top of one of the tower's roofs of this building lays a Blaire, a
scrawny-looking woman with brown hair tied in low pigtails, a rosy
complexion, and wearing a pink cotte with copper bracelets on her wrists
embedded with pink tourmaline. Around her waist hang an assortment of
pouches and a whip tied fast.

Her strange magenta-hued eyes look off into the horizon as she comfortably
hides high above and away. Away from her responsibilities in the team and
from people who calls her lazy - but that doesn't matter, not one bit to her,

what they think. The work they assign her is too tedious, so she'd rather not bother doing it.

Seeing something moving towards the fort piques her interest. Stretching a bit, she stirs and moves to the roof's edge. Taking out a telescope, Blaire points it down to study the object of her curiosity.

Her face lights up at what she sees.

It is Kaylan. He is back, and….. it looks like he brought along some kind of snobbish-looking, pointy-eared fellow. It must be a recruit he picked up on his outing.
Kaylan looks a bit beat up, so it must have been tough. At least, it appears he brought something back. You better head down and welcome them, then.

Opening a small pink portal with a small gesture, she leaps through it gleefully.

Walking along the path, Kaylan leads the way as he asks a bombardment of questions. Curious of everything about this elf and the realm he came from. "Uh….. your Highness, I was just wondering; I just read about your realm: is it really as cold and frigid there as in the books ?"

"No….. at least it's not like that, at least not throughout the entire year."

"How is realm travel? I always wanted to use it, but getting a traveler's stone is a tad bit expensive?" Kaylan throws another question.

"Vast, strange, starry filled, with a golden sea…. not much to talk about in my opinion." He tries getting over another one of his inquiries as fast as they approach their destination.

"Yet… I would think you would not come here on your own. Shouldn't you have come with some sort of escort? Considering being someone of your status." He asked him again.

"Just decided to come to slay this monster on your own power, so I just have to find a guide and some support to take on the chimera's minions; it's just not worth bringing my guards with me; that would have just been overkill," Atgeir says confidently, getting a bit annoyed at the elf.

"You must have lived for more than a century? I believe I heard elves live ten times longer than humans. You must be more than two hundred years of age, so do you know why your realm closed their gate?" He asks him yet another question, this one infuriating Atgeir. "More and more sulfren's poured in from other known realms, re-enforcing the one already left behind in our realm…. something bad happened…. someone important was lost because of it…. that's all to it, creature." He says coldly.

"Right…. still, can you please not call me creature. I gave you my name, and I am not just some unknown creature but a puca…. A type of shapeshifter… Some are troublemakers, but I am not like that….. I am an intellectual, you see……" He timidly tries to clarify himself to Atgeir as a small pink portal opens above him.

Blaire falls out of the portal right on top of him, knocking him down to the floor with a thud. "Hey Kay, you took your time getting back!" She shouts out at Kaylan, standing on top of him. "Kamaria was trying to get me to assist her with some research stuff….." Blaire continues on, not noticing she is still on Kaylan. "Blaire, can you please…. get off of me." He asks her weakly.

Blaire steps off hastily, a bit embarrassed that she forgot she was still on top of him. "Oh… uh, sorry about that there." She says, grinning sheepishly. As Kaylan gets up, she slowly shifts her gaze to a confused-looking Atgeir, unsure of what happened.

"Right, you must be a new recruit. So…. Uh, welcome to the Arcana regiment." She says, extending a hand to shake. Atgeir glares at it before looking her in the eyes, harshly correcting her. "Recruit! I am no new recruit to be initiated in your little group. I am Prince Atgeir Solstris, heir to the Severne Realm, and I am paying for your services to find and slay the Blood chimera, not to just be ordered around by some commoners."

With these words, her expression changes. "Oh, as if that matters when it comes to working with us. Besides, I can tell now you are…" She glares bitterly, pointing at Atgeir.

Kaylan goes behind him, gesturing desperately for her to cut it out. "…A pompous royal snob who is just going to make things more difficult for everyone here!" unable to stop her rant at him.

"You are going to regret saying that!" He gets into a fighting stance.

"Really, like that's going to happen!" She sneers spitefully back.

Kaylan backs away from them as a horrible headache develops, and he sees a flash of light. He looks on, frightened at what is about to happen.

In the fort's courtyard, throwing obsidian knives at a target pinned to a tree, a young man with short shaved blonde hair dressed in a loose-fitting white tunic stands with his hazel eyes focused on the target. He conjures a new knife in a puff of smoke in his gloved hand every time he throws one, his gloves made of black leather with copper studded and embedded with small Tanzanite.

Taking some time off to try to have a bit of fun. "Fritz, I see you are doing some recreational activity." He hears Kamaria, the team's assigned commander, behind him and turns around to see her standing against a pillar. Her black hair is tied up in a bun, and she is wearing a traditional yellow and grey patterned kanga dress, unique to her world, the Kusini realm, with brass bracelets embedded with topaz on both wrists, and her dark skin is painted with beautiful designs. "Still, I prefer to just read in my spare time… then throw daggers at a target pinned to a tree… something that involves more thought is much more appealing to me."

"You got something for me to do, Kam?" He asks her with a brow raised.

"Yes, but do I really only come to you… when I need something done from?" Kamaria says, smirking a tad. "Sure, why would you. You hang out with brainy folks like your little pal Kaylan." Fritz says, making her smile a bit at his comment.

"I sense trouble nearby; it seems Blair is fighting someone near the fort; it seems Kaylan is there as well. It looks like he came back from his outing." She explains the situation to him. Fritz just shrugs. "Do they really need some extra help with this? I'm sure they can deal with it themselves."

"I am certain I haven't sensed this kind of mana aura before; I want to see what it is - besides, it might be an entertaining fight." She reasons with him. Fritz's face lights up at this. "That's a different matter then. Come on, Kam. No time to waste just standing around here doing nothing!" He says enthusiastically, running past her.

Kamaria quickly sprints along, right behind him.

She is holding tightly onto her whip's handle with both hands that she has used to tie Atgeir's arms to his head, her boot pushing slightly against his forehead, holding him in place, her sleeves burnt and torn. The land scorched around them, with Kaylan to the side, transformed into a white wolf with his ears back and fur on end.

"Let go of me, you stinking human, or you'll regret it!" He yells back at her, struggling to break free. "I'll let you go when you...." She tiredly tries to make a witty comeback. She freezes as she feels a hand on her shoulder. "Curious, I am here to help, and it seems you did well enough on your own?" Kamaria says while inspecting developments. "Uh.... yea, I really had no problem dealing with him. You really had no reason to come.... to check up on me, Kam." Blaire responds, sounding quite tired.

"Good then.... no matter, I came here more to inspect this new type of mana aura I was sensing," she concludes, giving a cheeky little smile.

"I didn't; a nice fight would have elevated today." Fritz swaggers by complaining loudly. "I am sure you will get to fight again soon," Kamaria assures him. Sitting down next to Kaylan. "Great, it's better." He says before turning his attention to him. "....Oh, Kay.... there you are..... are you going to transform back now."

In a puff of smoke, he changes back to his standard form, his head lowered, feeling embarrassed that he did nothing to stop Blaire from fighting Atgeir. "I should go and explain things to Kamaria." Kaylan says, watching them, believing they should be responsible for telling her.

Fritz just nods as he lays on the ground.

"You must be the leader; I can see it. Tell your subordinate to let go of me." Atgeir tries to get Kamaria to do something to get him loose, but she is too distracted analyzing him. "An elf... never thought I would see one in person, and a quite tall one by that, or is that common among elves.... uh, by the burned area and the lingering feeling of electricity in the air, I say he uses electromancy..... his arcane weapon, is clawed silver gauntlets, strange, never saw silver used as a magical conductor for lightning before.... Thought silver was excellent at absorbing mana externally in fights, making it take longer to get fatigued. The bloodstone will give spells more of a power boost and tint the electricity scarlet red. It's actually...." snapping out of her rambling as Atgeir yells at her again. "Are you actually ignoring me? Tell this maniac to let me go; you can't just ignore me; I am.....!"

"Blaire, can you please let go of the elf. I am sure we can talk things out peacefully." She orders Blaire. She just lets go of him reluctantly, taking her foot off his back and letting loose her whip to take it off.

Atgeir stumbles forward, regaining his composure as he turns around to look furiously at them both. Kaylan rushes in between them to try to set things right. "Kamaria, I can explain things." He says, watching intently for her reaction.

"Go on then." She edges him on to give his explanation. "Right, I was testing a beast sample I acquired earlier when a terror beast snuck up on me. I couldn't beat it and was about to die when Prince Atgeir slayed the beast.... So we talked, and he told me he came to slay a monster called the Blood Chimera, a monster that seems to be orchestrating the terror beast invasion; he knows a lot about it. I made a deal to work for him to help and stop the beast for a reward." He says to her, adding a few more details through telepathy, which they are both well trained in order to communicate in secret and sometimes just ask each other complicated riddles for fun. {He might be horrible and egocentric, but I am sure this team-up will lead to the end of this terror beast threat, trust me.}

Kamaria responds assuredly back telepathically. {Certainly, I trust your judgment. We need to resolve this scuffle with Blaire before we can even think about doing this.}

Looking past him, she tells Atgeir, "Your Highness, I guess we owe you an apology for Blaire's actions. Be assured she will be harshly disciplined for it, appropriately."

"That's not fair, he started it. Why don't you….!" She yells out, objecting to Kamaria. {Please don't make this harder; we have a plan. Just play along. You won't be punished for this; we just need him to think that is it.} She sends a message to her mind to stop her, and she listens even though she would rather not. She hopes that Kamaria knows what she is getting into. "I didn't mean to say that… I am deeply… Sorry." She says with difficulty, giving her a quick bow before sitting next to Fritz.

"Perfect, I hope things will go smoother from here on... without any more incidents." Atgeir says gladly. "So follow me then. We shall discuss this in further detail. Plan out clearly what our next step will be." Kamaria responds, gesturing towards the fort's direction. Atgeir takes her offer, glaring back at Blaire smugly before going off with Kamaria and Kaylan to their base.

Blaire and Fritz still staying behind. "That lousy… royal.. snob, what in the world is Kamaria thinking. Trying to to…. ugh !" She yells out with them out of earshot. "Hey, don't get bent out of shape, B. There is nothing we can do about it." Fritz tells her nonchalantly.

"Why not ?!" She yells angrily at him.

"Just saying I got a fun way to get some payback without getting caught." He says, grinning widely. "What do you have in mind ?" She asks. "Let's just say when it comes to pranks, I can't be beat. Just say it is going to be quite entertaining." He tells her cheekily.

Both of them start laughing at the thought. "That's sounds great, you somewhat brilliant goofball…." Blair says before she suddenly collapses because of the exhausting battle, surprising Fritz. "The fight got you quite tired then, fine…. come on then, this ain't the best place to nap." He says, picking her up to carry over his shoulder, finally walking along slowly up the hill towards the fort as well.

CHAPTER 9
This is our plan

Back in the Hyvits Palace, the next day in the Severne realm, Sia stands before her son's room, accompanied by Aada, looking to say goodbye before being taken to the dreadful abyss defense tower. She still does not fully agree with her husband's decision, but when he is set on something, there is no talking him out of it. Gently, she knocks on the door before opening it carefully. "Good morning, my son…" She cheerfully chirps as she enters the room….. stunned to find he isn't there.

Walking around the room, she wonders if they had taken him away earlier than she had been told. Aada walks past her into the room to lean against a wall, sighing… "I can't believe Father sent Atgeir away earlier…. Mother, he's going to be gone for ages…. I didn't even get to say goodbye." Aada says, looking down sadly. "Couldn't we just go to the defense tower and see him real quick ?" She looks back up, asking her mother.

"Sorry, my dear, but that is out of the question; your father won't allow that. He has decided to keep us from contact as part of Atgeir's ordeal for his transgression."

"Why is father even going this far with this?" She asks while frantically creating a small, delicate, interlocking sphere of yellow light in her hand, trying to keep herself from stressing out.

Moving slowly out of the room, Sia gently grabs her shoulder as she tries to get past. "He just wants the best for him…. being the heir to the throne, he must be an example of the best of the best…. he just.." Sia struggles to say it. "Mother, you don't have to try to justify it…. I will see you later for your healing magic practice." Aada says, going away, leaving her mother in Atgeir's room.

Stunned, she stays there momentarily, going to his bed to sit on it to clear her head a bit.

Against the bed's post, something catches her attention from the corner of her eyes. A piece of paper poking from underneath the pillow. Leaning over, she removes it from under it, opening it up to read its contents.

Reading it over, her face slowly shifts to an expression of great concern, increasing with every written word.

Mother, this letter is left for your eyes only, where I knew you'd find it.

This is written to give some clarity on why I just left.

I will be gone; I don't know for how long, and I am not telling where. Rest assured that when I have accomplished what I have set out to do. My legacy will be sealed for millenniums to come. My skills are more than sufficient to clear any opposition I will encounter.

Clutching the paper against her chest, she wonders what Atgeir was trying to do. He seems confident in what he has planned.

Just have to keep this from Eilif for now… she can't bear hiding things from her husband, yet she won't have to keep it hidden for ages as Sia assures herself that she will tell him when it appears Atgeir's quest is taking far too long. She wants him to succeed, but not at the risk of him getting hurt or worse… she won't lose him, too. Hastily, she goes over to the closet, slipping it in behind it; it's a good hiding spot for the time being.

Unaware of Thyra peering in on her. Watching her intently, hidden behind the other side of the room entrance.

As a day begins back in Atgeir's home realm, a day starts to come to an end in the Thiar realm.

In an office lit by the setting sun, stacks of books, vials, and crystal tool boxes littering the room, Kamaria sits behind an old oak desk with Kaylan standing beside her, Atgeir sitting in front of it, telling her what this blood chimera is, what it looks like and how it is connected to all of this. "Still not sure why none of your team knows anything of this; someone from this realm did send us a telepathic message… Not sure how I presume a human can't even get it right to accomplish such a feat, but then again, I wouldn't be here if I hadn't gotten one." He concludes his explanation to both of them.

"What do you mean, we weren't told any of this…. this person who sent you this could not be associated with us… still, why won't they share this information." Kamaria says with an open book lying in front of her. "This fellow could be a member of the Radiant Knights brotherhood; they have been absent through the invasion… They are quite secretive and distrust our king and anyone associated with him like us, but it could have been a last-ditch distress message to anyone outside the realm to intervene…. at least it is a theory for now." Kaylan chips in with a lengthy suggestion.

"Sounds like about right." Kamaria comments, setting her eyes back onto Atgeir. "But the who gave the information doesn't matter now." She states while flipping through the book's pages to a specific one. Scanning it quickly. "Your description of the monster does match with recent sightings of this monster thought; it appears to have appeared during an attack on Comfrey village… Watching everything occur from a far-off hill flew off when some of the regiment fighters approached it, uninterested in interacting with them, they reported it back to us….. we didn't think much of it at the time." She says, giving Atgeir a lead.

"It flew off, so where is it now, then?" He asks her.

"It appears to revisit Comfrey village often, skulking nearby. Every time it flies off as someone gets too close, we don't know where it goes when it flies off to, but there is a high chance we might find it if we go visit this village, as it seems it wants to be seen... at the very least." She gives him further details and lays out a route. She closes her book and places it back in the desk drawer.

"Great, well done, then you will take me there first thing tomorrow. I suspect you will provide me with etiquette sleeping arrangements for someone of my status." Atgeir informs them what exactly he wants from them.

"Of course, You can have the commander's quarters." She offers it, getting attention from Kaylan. {Do you really want to give up your room? You will have to share a quarter with Blaire.} He asks her telepathically, not wanting Atgeir to hear it. {It's all fine; I have no problem with sharing quarters with Blaire… besides, I am sure she would enjoy a bit of intellectual conservation with me, for once.} She reassures him. {I am not so sure about that, but if you are okay with it, I am.} He nods at her as he concludes their telepathic conversation. Kamaria looks past Atgeir, waiting impatiently, straight at the door. "I will get you someone to take you to your room." She tells him.

{Fritz, come in; I know you there, and please, don't try anything.} She sends him a command.

Fritz strides in, standing next to Atgeir. "Fritz, take Prince Atgeir to the commander's quarters." Kamaria tells him what to do. "Sure thing, Kam." He says, quickly saluting, leading Atgeir out of the room.

"That went fantastically…. well, considering what happened prior," Kaylan says with a deep sigh.

"I wish you could have talked them out of fighting in the first place." Kamaria adds. "I do too; it's just like when I fight…. I feel this terrible headache along with a flash of a…. a memory, ugh… then I start to reme..." He tries to tell her.

"You don't have to tell me. We tried to have this conversation before; you don't have to bring it up until you're ready." She says to him kindly with a smile. "Thanks…. uh….. again." He lets her know.

"It's never a problem. You are the first friend I made when I came to this realm…. We are and always will be fellow apprentices of Master Glynn." She says, getting up to place her hand on his shoulder. They give each other a friendly glance.

Fritz Stands by the open door, showing him the room. "There you go, your quarters for the stay." Letting Atgeir pass him into the room to look around it. "Oh… one thing, just watch out for the bedbugs in this realm, we call them…. Mega biters. They are quite big, and it's bite… Horrible. See you tomorrow, Atdy." Fritz says mischievously and mockingly, trying not to laugh.

"What did you just say?!" Atgeir yells out, horrified by what he heard. He turns around to find Fritz is nowhere to be found; he must have run off. Good then, after he addressed him so disrespectfully, Atgeir scoffs at the very thought. "The nerve him of that discourteous cretin." He mutters to himself, sure he is just trying to mess with him.

Closing up the room's door. Atgeir goes to sit down on the bed. It feels uncomfortable. The room feels tiny with all these towers of books and other clutter everywhere, like in that office; their leader must be some kind of know-it-all bookworm to hoard all this in such a manner. Still, he won't have to stay in this cramped old place for long, he reassures himself.

It might have started badly, but Atgeir is confident that things will improve. Funny, he snickers. Leifur would have enjoyed going on this quest; he was always so adventurous and beyond reckless. Atgeir wonders what Leifur would think of him going on such a treacherous adventure; he ponders as he recalls a memory.

CHAPTER 10
Remembering the far past

A hundred and eleven years ago, in the Severne realm ...

It's in the midst of winter, and the palace's garden is covered in snow. Sprinting through the grounds, a much younger Atgeir. Just a child with his face clear, without the scar under his eyes. Going through, underneath a wide canopy covered in flowering vines where his mother is sitting with Aada drinking tea on a marble bench, to skipping across the stones on the half-frozen pond, to sprinting around his father discussing something with the Crows, the old Nerium still being among them, without bothering them, going further away. He goes on a slow walk and stops at a massive singular tree at the far end of this vast garden. Looking around it to try and find his brother, he said he would be here to show him something.

Searching around the tree for him, finding seven small logs propped up on poles of different heights. This wasn't here yesterday.

Snap!….

He hears a loud sound of bolts past him as one of the logs shatters; Atgeir stumbles back in fright as he hears more sudden loud bursts.

..Snap!…

Another one shatters…

…..Snap!..

As one more of the log shatter, looking up, he sees a shadow bolting across the tree's branches as it leaps down in front of him with a dramatic bow to reveal that it is Leifur. "And that's what I called an amazing entrance." He exclaims enthusiastically, his dark hair in a wild mess with leaves sticking out of it. Looking on at an appalled Atgeir.

"Would have been better if you didn't look like you just slept a night up a tree and were attacked by a group of aggravated squirrels; that isn't a good look for the heir to the throne, maybe… I should get it instead... I am way more ambitious and assertive than you… instead of some carefree, adventurous type." Atgeir comments smugly with a smirk, confident in his statement.

Leifur laughs at the thought, stroking back his hair to get the leaves out of it. "Really, maybe you could. Then I might go on a crazier scenario than the one you thought up, like a realm trip." Leifur says half-jokingly and half-seriously to Atgeir.

"Sure… as if that would happen.. like a father would just let his prodigal son go off on some wild escapade to some far-off world." Atgeir replies in his own joking manner.

"Yeah, that is… kind of a problem, but you aren't here to discuss that, Geir." Leifur says, pointing his hand to one of the logs. "I asked you to come here to show you my new amazing spell and how it is done." He snaps his finger, shooting off a powerful sound bullet to its target, shattering the log into splinters. "I call it the sound wave blast, part of like a new type of branch of enchantment magic, I am inventing…. don't really have a name for it at the moment…. but if I can get a musical instrument like a flute or a rebec to do more complex spells, it will be fun to use in combat." Leifur tells him excitably. "I can just concentrate my mana at a single point and then release it when I make a sound, sending it through it to create a powerful sound wave; fantastic, ain't it?" He explains it while making the snapping gesture he made earlier.

"Where will you get time to learn this new magic branch? Isn't Father strongly set on training you in pyromancy?" Atgeir questions him.

"Like that is going to stop me from doing it, from going after what I want to do. I can always just sneak out into the forest to work on it at night, and I am sure I can get an instrument from somewhere. Then it will truly be amazing… he won't know a thing." He says, without a single bit of doubt in his tone. Holding up his fists in the air in deviance.

Atgeir lowers his head a moment, a big grin spreading on his face. "That all sounds like a challenge. You got some new powerful spells you're working on, but wait until I start my arcane combat training with electromancy. Then, I'm going to surpass you fast." He responds back confidentially.

"Really, I better step up then." Leifur tells him, giving him a light-hearted jab to the shoulder. Atgeir punches back harder, catching Leifur off by surprise, but he laughs at it while Atgeir wipes off the spot clean Leifur hit him.

"We should get inside to prepare for dinner. The noble Lysar family is coming over for dinner…" Atgeir mentions to him. His brother is certainly done showing off his new spell. "Yeah, I forgot they were coming over… Why are you in a rush though to see them…. I know you like to hang out at lavish get-togethers with other royalty and nobility… to try and show off… how…." Leifur wonders a bit. "Oh… Now I get it; you are excited to see Revna again." He says cheekily.

"No, not at all. Revna being there has nothing to do with it…." Atgeir says, looking slightly away from Leifur's gaze to hide his slight blush, brought up by the thought of her.

"Sure… Sure…. not at all." Leifur says, getting Atgeir to turn his gaze to him as he leaps back up into the tree. "I'm just going out for a bit, Geir. I will return before mother or father even notice I was gone." He yells out to Atgeir down there.

"Leifur, if you come back late, I'm telling on you… I'm going to hold you getting caught, over you for years and years, brother…" He yells back, not interested in having this event to be stopped to look for Leifur because of the remaining sulfrens roaming all over the realm. "Like I am going to end up coming back late, for you to even get to do that." He says further up the tree before jumping over and across the wall, out of sight.

Atgeir laughs a bit at the memory, laying restfully on the bed, his gauntlets on the nightstand with the backpack hanging from it.

He barely got back that day; he showed up in a hurry. He told Atgeir afterward that he ran into a sulfren while going to a village to get an instrument. He didn't have to go out to get one; they had musical instruments stored somewhere in the palace he could get, but Leifur was always the one to take the most dangerous route to his objective. He guessed Leifur just liked the thrill of it more, but Atgeir never got why it was fun, though.

He wonders as he drifts off… Wishing that his brother was still here….

CHAPTER 11
Heading off to Comfrey village

Silently crouched down next to a door and listening intently to hear through it, Blaire and Fritz look at each other. Both of them smile widely, filled with anticipation of what is going to happen this morning.

"Any minute now." Fritz says quietly, standing a bit up to look through the door's keyhole, seeing Atgeir still fast asleep. Giving Blaire a chance to peak in, she also notices a flock of sparrows pecking away at seeds on the floor. "What's with the birds? It's a nuisance and all, but how will it really get him back for what he did to him?" She asks in a hushed whisper.

"It's just part of it… only a part of it, B." He tells her assuredly. "Besides, you're about to see it in about…. three…. two…. one." He says while counting down on his fingers.

At the count of one, a drop of water falls out of a small crack from the ceiling onto Atgeir's face, waking him up. His movement startles a dog sleeping underneath the bed, making it jolt up, knocking him into the flock of birds.

Atgeir tries desperately to get up in a flurry of flapping wings, walking right onto a weight-activated platform hidden by the birds. Making a bucket of sticky tree sap splash out over him along with the bucket followed shortly behind it, hitting him on the head. He looks around, confused and furious at his surroundings.

Both Fritz and Blaire erupt in laughter, alerting Atgeir of their presence. "There you are, you scoundrels !" He yells out, coming at the door.

"It's time to scram, Fritzy." Blaire hastily creates a portal, dragging Fritz through with her. Gone, as Atgeir slams the door open to find the culprits nowhere to be found. Frustrated and covered in sap, he slams the door shut again to try and clean himself from the mess. Thinking the whole time that when he finds the ones who did this to him, they will regret it deeply.

Fritz and Blaire watch all this happen, hidden behind a corner further down the hallway, snickering quietly at Fritz's humorous plan succeeding.

Drinking a large cup of coffee, Kamaria enjoys a quizzical conversation with Kaylan in the courtyard, sitting at an old wooden table. As the rest of the regiment members go about their daily tasks, they walk past to get to where they must go. Fritz comes running in with Blaire, smiling widely at each other as they go past them. "You two seem to be in a good mood. Did anything interesting happen?" Kamaria asks them. Fritz just looks back with his hand against the side of his face; he gives a vague answer in turn. "B and I just had a bit of fun starting off the day on a high note. Went to play around with the dog and an entire flock of somewhat friendly sparrows; it was quite entertaining indeed…. till the birds turned on us all at once at the end." Blaire nods frantically in agreement with his explanation. "That sounds…. like an interesting activity…. I would have enjoyed being there to witness it," Kamaria comments, a bit suspicious of what they were up to.

"You really missed out, I would love to stay and talk about it, but I have to go do something with B…. so… uh… see you later." He lets her know, trying to walk away. "Oh, I have something to tell you before you go." Kamaria calls out to Fritz, stopping him in his tracks. "Just don't take too long; you are going to come with us to Comfrey village on a mission with Atgeir." She tells him.

"What about me? Why aren't you taking me with you?" Blaire yells out, questioning why she is being left behind.

"Because we are trying to make Atgeir think you are going through some kind of punishment for what you did to him. So your job is to keep out of sight for a while." Kamaria tells her calmly. "Fine, I understand, but you will definitely regret it; you would have gotten there faster with my portals." She retorts, storming off, annoyed. Fritz shrugs as he falls in behind her, going with Blaire to try and cheer her up.

"I think we should check on Prince Atgeir; he did seem in a hurry to slay that monster as fast as possible…. I think Fritz and Blair might have done something mischievous." Kaylan suggests.

"I thought the same; they must have gotten some revenge for what happened. Blaire can't let something like that go, and Fritz won't let a friend go it alone." Kamaria agrees. "Better clear things up with him then." She stands up, gesturing for Kaylan to go and see Atgeir.

With all the creatures kicked out of the room, Atgeir meticulously finishes himself up for the day. He used a combination of electrical and wind spells to forcefully blast the sap off of him all across the room, making it more of a mess than it was, but that didn't matter if he ended up having to stay in this realm longer than he had hoped for. He ponders as he ties his hair back neatly. Atgeir decides he just has to pay to stay at some inn; anything would be better than being here with these hooligans and their barn they call a fort.

He would still keep them as his new underlings as he sees it but would rather not sleep in this place.

He looks in a mirror on the wall to see if his face is still dirty from that incident. Cleaning up smudges on his skin and flattening back stray hairs.

Knock….. knock…… knock………

They have arrived … Atgeir opens the door to see Kamaria there with Kaylan behind her. "I see you had a rough morning; it appears the sparrows got in again. They tend to fly in from holes in the fort's walls." Kamaria says, trying to dispel any thoughts that Fritz or Blaire did this. "And how did the mutt that was under the bed get in?" Atgeir asks coldly, irritated.

"Oh…. you must mean Fergal; he must have slipped in and fell asleep before you came in yesterday." She answers confidentially.

"You can explain that, but this was certainly orchestrated. I'm sure that…. what is one dressed in pink named…. Be…Ble…. Bleeny…." He tries to recall her name but fails. "Whatever her name was, the bucket of sap and the contraption attached to it." Atgeir tells her fiercely.

With this, Kaylan chips in. "It was a prank done by our very own Blaire and Fritz, but it… was intended for…. uh, Kamaria. Set up long before your arrival over a disagreement." He places his hand on the back of his head. "I kind of… forgot all about it after all the recent events." Kaylan says a bit nervously.

Kamaria smiles at this fabricated story, knowing that he wouldn't let it happen to her, but Atgeir doesn't. "Quite appalling; my sympathies for bringing you knowingly into this trap." Kaylan says, trying to smile as sincerely as Kamaria is.

Glancing at the messed-up quarters, he looks skeptically back at Kamaria. Sure, both of them are making all this up, but time is of the essence, and he would want to finish this quest as fast as possible to then deal with these humans and…. the puca creature. "That is quite behind us now….. but that is the prime reason we work together." Atgeir says, keeping his anger somewhat hidden in his tone and getting confused looks from them. "You must have come to get me so we can go to this village where the chimera was seen, right." He continues, going right to the terms of their alliance.

"Of course, we were just about to get the horses ready. Just say the word, and we're off." Kamaria replies swiftly.

"Then get a move on, I don't have time to just stand about your stable." Atgeir snaps back.

"Alright then." Kamaria says as she walks away with both Kaylan and Atgeir. "Kaylan, go and get Fritz." She orders him as they continue down the hallway, and he nods and hurriedly runs off to find him.

Resting alongside the tranquil river, only a short distance from the fort. Blaire lays down on her back on the soft grass; she laughs loudly as she thinks back at the prank she pulled off with Fritz. "We really got that rude snob, good… Fritzy, that was a hilarious bit of payback." Blaire tells him smugly. Placing her hands behind her head, grinning, she looks over to Fritz, who is skillfully twirling a dagger about in his hand. "I would say it was mostly me who pulled that prank off. You just assisted, but that is just what I think." Fritz nonchalantly comments on her statement, throwing his dagger into the air. It spins around before vanishing into a puff of smoke. "Hey, I helped a lot with preparing that prank. Teleporting birds into those quarters wasn't easy; they wouldn't willingly fly into some strange glowing portal." Blaire responds, offended he would remark that she didn't contribute much to their payback plan.

"I can agree to that, B. You put more effort into this than you usually do… with anything that involves putting any actual work in." Fritz says, placing his hand on top of Blaire's head as he leans against her. "Yeah, sure... really funny, absolutely hilarious." She remarks sarcastically, shoving him off of her.

 "Thanks very much; I pride myself on my great sense of humor." Fritz says with a wide cheeky grin, unfazed by what she just said, giving a quick bow. Blaire cocks her head to the side, looking on at him with a frown, unimpressed by his attitude. "You know I didn't mean it, I was just being sarcastic." She speaks up spitefully, crossing her arms. "I know, I just don't really care…." Fritz answers smugly, putting his hands behind his head. "I just had some fun this morning and now have something nice to look at on the regiment's next quest…. things are going great for me." Fritz clarifies in a relaxed manner, chuckling slightly. Confusing Blaire even more with what he's even talking about. "I don't get it; what are you going on about…. what nice-looking thing are you….." She asks in a baffled tone, interrupted by a distant call.

"Fritz…. Fritz, it's time... We're heading out right now!" Kaylan shouts as he runs down the hill towards them, getting Fritz and Blaire's attention. "See ya later, B." Giving a quick salute to her before he runs off to meet the puca. "Wait, you haven't answered my question yet !" Blaire yells out to him, bolting up to her feet. Fritz stops in his tracks, looking back. "Let me think about it….. no, leaving you guessing is far more fun…. for me." He says, grabbing onto Kaylan. He runs off toward the fort. "Seriously, you can't really… you can't just leave me like that….." She shouts back at him till he is out of her sight. Feeling frustrated, Blaire kicks at the ground, hitting a rock into the lake. She's not going to stay back at Fort Borage after that. Blaire will just have to go along; they won't even know. Smiling mischievously, Blaire creates a portal right next to her, and she swiftly leaps through.

At the fort's stables, Kamaria and Atgeir stand next to the horses. "Why do you treat your subordinates in such a casual manner?" He asks her, feeling curious about the subject. "It was how the one I and Kaylan were apprentice to treated us, so I think it might have rubbed off on me, and now it is how I lead." She responds cheerfully, getting a disgusted look from Atgeir. "That sort of attitude will just make you seem a pushover to your underlings, some kind of friend to toy with." He says he is sure that his stance is correct.

"That sounds like a horrible way to see things." Kamaria says, unfazed, as he glares at her. They hear the distant sound of a door opening, looking over to see Kaylan walking out from the building with Fritz beside, reluctantly following.

"Didn't think you'd call for me, so darn fast." Fritz says as he walks up to her, Kaylan going past him to stand beside Kamaria. "Good, you're here." She exclaims, going over to get up on one of the horses. "Right, everyone, saddle up; we're heading out." She calls out. All of them get on a horse except for Kaylan. Atgeir is next to him, looking down at him. "Why haven't you taken a horse? Do you think you can run all the way to the village?" Atgeir asks Kaylan, snickering a bit at him.

"You don't know… pucas can shape-shift into about four different animals, one of them being a horse." He says, transforming into a pure white stallion in a burst of smoke. Atgeir looks on, surprised, as he gallops off with his mind orb, flying off speedily after him; Atgeir looks on as the other two follow.

He sighs as it sinks in that he will have to deal with more of this. He rides off, joining in after them.

CHAPTER 12
Our time in Comfrey village

Looking down from the fort's roof as they ride away, Blaire sits crossed-legged. They left, thinking she was just going to stay behind. As if that is going to happen, and she is certain Fritz knows it!

Seeing they are now out of sight, she opens up one of her portals and goes through to climb out of another portal further away from the fort. Making a new portal as she goes further and further. Her portals have a maximum range she can teleport, but with this method, she can get to where they are going before her mana runs out and ends up unable to even move. Through her multiple teleportations, she notices a strange, small, dark figure flashing past her in the corner of her view. Is something following her? She peaks up her speed to try and get rid of it.

It stays in her sight, and she goes even faster, yet it still keeps up. What in the world is this thing following her? There is only one way to find out then.

Coming to a quick halt and looking back, she faces her pursuer, making it stop dead in its tracks as she did.

Her face changes to an expression of disbelief, stunned to see what stands before her. "What in all the known realms even are you?!"

Riding the horses in full gallop across the path near white and red flower-covered fields, they can see a flock of sheep grazing calmly in the field.

Crossing a stone bridge, they slow down as they approach a steep hill leading up to the village. As they reach the top, they are met with a horribly…. terrible sight…. Comfrey village is…. is in ruins: buildings with holes bashed in them, slain terror beasts of all sorts of terrifying appearances, and injured guards and some of the members of the Arcana regiment. Frightened villagers looking on at all of this, still not recovered from what just happened, and the realization of their destroyed homes.

Among them is a figure clad in an orange and brown cloak, his hood over his head and his face hidden by a dark wooden mask, a strange green glow emanating from this mask's eyes. Going about, crouched over a guard… healing him with his hands on the wound, glowing.

Transforming back, Kaylan goes off to help heal people with Kamaria, who leaps off her horse, running to an Arcana regiment sorcerer. "What happened here? How did this happen?" She asks concerned. "The terror beasts…. attacked the village at first light; we weren't prepared at all." He replies, holding his pained head up with his hand. "We would have all perished if not for that one over there." He points weakly at the cloaked fellow.

"Thank you, you said enough. Get some rest, my friend." She says warmly, getting up and walking over to the cloaked figure.

Extending her hand to him, Kamaria greets him. "Good afternoon, sir. I was told you are the one to thank for stopping this attack." The cloaked one looks up at her. "It wasn't a problem at all." He says happily.

"You might not think so, but I am certain everyone can agree that you did tremendous thing… You could join the Arcana regiment; we need more people like you." Kamaria replies, giving a warm smile. "I appreciate the offer but think I would do better alone." He says, confident of his point.

"That's quite the shame, but I think…. I understand." She says.

He stands up confidentially, giving a suggestion. "What do you say? After everyone is healed, we scrounge up a few things and have little uplifting occasions to lift everyone's spirits so they can move on … I am sure the Arcana regiment would want to do something to help out… This does seem early…" He tells her his plan, stopping abruptly as he sees Atgeir approaching them. "What are you two conversing about?" He asks Kamaria.

"Just a little discussion on joining everyone here for an entertaining gathering to make everyone feel better." She lets him know. "Have you forgotten I'm short on time to slay the Blood chimera?" He retorts coldly at this. Raising a brow, she sighs, ready to try to say something, but seeing this, the cloaked one gives an answer. "I think I know what beast you're talking about; if you stay a bit longer here, I can tell you where I saw it went." He says.

He looks at this strange masked fellow, uncertain of his intention of wanting them to stay there longer, but he does seem to know something. "Fine… It beats scouring for a chance that it will show up again." He says bitterly. "Great, I am sure you and your friends will enjoy this breather, considering what you must overcome." He remarks, giving a gracious bow as he dashes off to continue healing the injured. "We sure will." Kamaria calls out before returning to Atgeir, whose sight is locked on the cloaked one.

"Did he give you a name ?" He asks without even looking at her. "No, I didn't even ask." She says, curious about why he wants to even know. "Why do you ask ?" She comes closer to him, trying to look him in the eyes.

He turns away from her. "Just a nagging feeling I have… he feels so familiar… ugh…. This just doesn't concern you the least." Atgeir says, quickly walking away from her.

Kamaria watches him leave, unsure what to make of this... what is he keeping from her.

On the other side of the village, Kaylan is busy healing a guard, his hands placed on a deep cut on his leg with a glowing purple aura enveloping the wound.

"This won't take much longer." Kaylan tells him as it slowly closes up in a moment. Looking at his healed spot, he gets up and extends his hand to the guard. Pulling him up as he grabs onto his hand. "Thank you, dearly." The guard says, not mentioning the fact a puca helped him.

The guard walks off, giving a quick wave. Now, for the next one, Kaylan reminds himself there is more to be done, but before he can even go to the next one, his mind changes as he spots someone the puca thought he would never see again. Frantically, Kaylan runs behind a crumbling wall, crouching down. He peers from behind it, hidden from the old man's view. Why is he here? This isn't the village he lived in; did he travel here for something. Ducking back behind in his hiding place, a bright flash of light flashes in front of his eyes like the ones he gets in stressful situations along with the headache. It's that horrible memory that is trying to resurface again in his mind, the one he is trying to lock away, and it's getting harder to suppress, more and more each day!

"Calm down… calm down….. just have to keep out of sight; he won't see me. We won't be here long…. he won't get me to remember that… he won't… I don't want to tell him… about that… no," He tries to reassure himself in a strained whisper as he lays his head against the wall.

Under a cloudless starry night, they set out a row of connected tables they brought out together in the center of the village, decorated with various colors of torn tablecloths. Placed on it is food made from what they could find in the rubble and some fish caught by the Kaylan and the cloaked one a few moments before; this feast consisted of cabbage soup, mashed potatoes with kale, roasted parsnips, barley bread, baked trouts with butter sauce and a two keg of whisky that wasn't completely damaged in the attack.

It took a while for the villagers to get into the spirit of things. Still, with Fritz's unbound enthusiasm, he sings a song, holding onto a glass of whisky, along with the masked one playing a strange a lute that has been painted in scarlet to appear to have eyes and sharp fangs; stranger enough it seems the eyes are following peoples movements as if it is alive. It is embedded with small clusters of emeralds on the instruments side with black steel lining it.

The sulfren scourge we beat
They down into the ground
Till there were none to be
Found by their now-powerless
Master's utmost profound
Yet a new threat arises with
Fang and claw drawn, ready
To slaughter but won't let them at their
Gruesome feast, for we will slay them
Down as the ones who tried ages ago

Fritz goes around the tables merrily, singing an upbeat tune while dancing about, shouting out how tough the people of the Thiar realm are compared to others. Atgeir watches him and the feast from afar, eating a piece of trout as he doesn't want to eat things with subpar ingredients. "Not hungry, I thought you'd taken more, considering you haven't eaten today." Kamaria asks him.

Turning his gaze to her, he replies. "Where I am from, we don't just scarf down copious amounts; we eat in small amounts with the meal being made of quality ingredients…. I am merely forcing myself to eat this… food." Looking at his fork.

Kamaria chuckles at this statement. "It's your choice. Still, you are missing out, though, on some delicious meals..... Considering all that happened, the villagers would be glad if you participated in this a little more. We need to help out, to lighten the mood.... Specifically." She gives him a lengthy explanation, getting a cold sneer back. Out of the corner of his eye, Atgeir notices the cloak one is walking away, out of the village. He Shoves his plate into Kamaria's hands. "Take this, I have something better to do." He says as he sprints off, going after the cloaked one.

"Where are you going?!" She yells out to him, getting no answer in return. Kamaria shakes her head, utterly unsurprised by this as he thinks so highly of himself that he won't hesitate to answer someone he considers below him. Kamaria goes to a table and places the plate down before walking to the side of the wrecked house, where Kaylan sits on the floor eating his food, trying to keep himself out of sight.

She sits beside him and gives him a reassuring smile, with Kaylan returning it. "I didn't feel like eating around all these people; I wanted some space." He says meekly, being not one for crowds. Kamaria nods knowingly at this, accepting this in parts, but she can't help but wonder if there is more to this.

CHAPTER 13
Discovering our next destination

The cloaked fellow walks through the dense forest as the sounds of the nighttime life echo through the trees and a gentle breeze blows through the night air. He heads to a clearing to stand next to a fallen tree and a boulder.

He looks ahead to the trees, seeing an owl perched comfortably on a branch. Walking around the fallen oak, he starts to whistle a tune.

"There you are." Atgeir whispers with a grin while holding high up onto a tree. Bursting forth from the darkness of night, a blinding fast Atgeir erupts from above, kicking the cloaked man down to the ground with a blow to the head. The cloaked figure stumbles away, a bit disorientated, his mask lying on the ground. He keeps his face concealed. Atgeir walks closer to him, combing back his hair with his fingers. "Let's see what you're hiding behind." He says cockily, but that attitude soon vanishes as the cloaked one turn his unmasked face towards him.

"This can't be… this just can't…. how can it even be…." Atgeir says shakily. He looks on in shock as the mysterious man pulls away his hood. This elf, with his short black hair and confident grey eyes, with the left one having a clawed scar running over it and another on his chin, has no mistaking it; it can't be anyone other than his older brother, Leifur!

"Surprise, Geir!" Leifur exclaims as he gets up, looking over at the absolutely stunned Atgeir, dumbfounded with a multitude of thoughts racing through his mind: how is he alive… why is he here… why in all the known realms, why didn't he come back… why…. why…..!?

"Knew you'd follow me, though I didn't think you would come in kicking me right in the head…" He goes on, stopped only by a sucker punch to the gut by Atgeir. "I should have kicked you harder for what you did." His brother shouts at him scornfully. Getting back his composure from the punch, Leifur speaks up, trying to calm the upset brother down. "I'm sorry for running away, but I couldn't just stay there, to be set for a boring life filled with endless responsibilities I never wanted. Besides, now you get to be the heir to the throne… isn't it what you always wanted."

Atgeir just retorts angrily with his fists clenched. "Yes, obviously!…. but that's not the point; I could become the realm's heir if you're there or not, I could have manipulated you out of it, so easily!… You took away a slightly better challenge to actually getting it….. this is all about your idiotic chase for a life of adventure… leaving behind your family and making us believe you were dead! You really hurt mother the most of us all!"

"I am sorry for what I did, but that doesn't change my decision to leave that life behind… yet I do regret not telling you that day that I was leaving the Severne realm… And that I would be fine." Leifur says, turning away. "Oh, I almost forgot, for honoring our deal….. the Blood Chimera was heading to Astera Bay, I am certain of that… and one more thing, I will see you there to finish this up when you think this whole thing more thoroughly through." He says before he sprints off.

"You're not going anywhere; we're not even close to done talking!" Atgeir yells, dashing after him, struggling to keep up with Leifur through the dense trees. His big brother gets further and further away until he is entirely out of sight. Falling to the ground, Atgeir furiously slams the ground with his fists, causing a burst of crimson lightning to shoot off around him, leaving the ground around him scorched and breaking a tree nearby in two.

Jumping back in fright at a loud thunderous clap, Blaire looks around nervously, with a strange creature holding onto her back with its bony-clawed hands. Its eyes are cavernous voids in its leathery purple spiked face, and it has a jagged smile with an orange glow coming from it. The thin rat-like body is adorned with multiple dark patterns. Protruding from its tail a bunch of luminescent tendrils. She decided to call it Dark, as it didn't seem to be able to talk or perhaps just didn't want to talk to her to tell its name.

Dark was the thing that was following her across her teleporting journey, and it immediately lashed onto her, sniffing her with its nostrils. Now she is with it and unable to get it loose, as it grips her unbelievably tight. Yet it seems harmless, so why bother any longer to try and pry it off, she believes.

Continuing cautiously into the forest, she wonders what had caused that loud noise. While sneaking around in the village, she overheard them having some kind of feast. They said they would later go and find the Blood Chimera because they got information from a guy on where it was. They were sure about leaving in the morning.

Quickly, Blaire creates a portal, jumps through it, and lands on a sturdy branch in a tree. Using her whip, she ties her waist to the branch to prevent her from falling off while she sleeps, lying down on her back. The creature still won't let go. This little spike covered monster isn't going to move an inch! This is going to be an uncomfortable sleeping arrangement, and that is saying something - she once fell asleep in a crate of bricks! The creature has an awfully eerie presence that just makes her feel so unnaturally cold. This is going to make her sleep even more uncomfortable.

Atgeir walks in. Everything is now completely silent. The tables are stacked with empty plates. Some villagers are slumped, sleeping on and around tables, with Fritz among them - resting on a tabletop, sprawled out on top of a large fellow. The rest are asleep in their broken houses.

"You're back. Done with what you went off to do?" Kamaria steps out from the shadow of a building. "I now know the location of the Blood Chimera... we're heading out immediately tomorrow, at first light." He says with a scowl, still bitter at his brother. "Right then... the destination is set... good we're closer to ending this." Kamaria replies cautiously, seeing the deep rage inside of him. She backs up, walking away from him back into the broken building with her curiosity more piqued at what just happened; there had to be more to his interaction with the cloaked fellow. Kamaria ponders as she lays down on a stack of hay, where Kaylan is sleeping perched on top of the roof, shape-shifted into the form of a pure white raven.

Atgeir sleeps a fair bit away from them in the village on a bed; he paid someone off, making them sleep somewhere on the ground in their own house.

CHAPTER 14
More questions and yet few answers

A hundred and ten years ago, in the Severne realm inside the Hyvits Palace.

A young Atgeir wears a glove made of leather and steel and embedded with clear gems on one of his hands - a practice arcane weapon before they get their actual one. He runs crouched low between the library bookcases, now and then peaking out from behind each corner, a small ball of electricity on the tip of one of his fingers ready to shoot. He is looking out for his opponent, Leifur, in this game.

Slam!.....

He looks back, frightened at the sound of books falling from the shelves. Was it him? No matter; he's not going to stay there to find out. Atgeir dashes off quickly, still keeping himself low to prevent being seen, sliding down under a table.

Watching intently from underneath it for any signs of Leifur.

He hears a loud snap as he feels a burst of force hit close to him. Crawling hurriedly back, he gets out from under the table. Rolling around, he rushes behind a bookcase. He peers out carefully to see Leifur standing on top of a bookcase on the other side of the library, wearing the same glove. Atgeir points his finger at him and shoots out a small bolt of lightning at him.

Leifur dodges it easily. Leaping down from the bookcase, he dashes towards Atgeir. Ready to use a sound spell to bash him. Atgeir runs off with his older brother in pursuit right behind him.

Atgeir notices a servsi walking ahead of him, and he grabs onto it as Leifur snaps his finger, launching another bolt. Blocking the attack with the Golem's tiny body, knocking the poor thing unconscious, he throws it right at his brother.

"That's not fair, Atgeir, using servsi's as shields - come on, that's what I call cheating!" Leifur says as he takes the time to place the servsi he caught gently on the floor. "Yes, it is, as long is it leaves to me winning it… then it's fair." Atgeir shouts out, now hiding in cover. The game's objective is to see who hits their opponent first with their best spell.

Atgeir climbs on top of the bookcase, running across it to get behind his brother, jumping off it with both hands electrified and ready to grab onto him. Sensing this, Leifur uses a quick upward kick in an arc, sending him flying into the bookcase and falling to the floor with a thud. Using this opportunity, Leifur snaps his finger, sending a small sound wave, hitting Atgeir in the stomach.

"And that makes me victorious!" Leifur yells out, throwing his fists into the air with a broad smile, basking in Atgeir's defeat. "I was holding back, you know." Atgeir weakly says as he stumbles back up, holding onto one of the bookcase's shelves nearby. "If I was really trying, you would have come short." He says, pointing at Leifur. "Really, do you want to do a rematch -

then you can show me how good you are?" His brother says smugly. Atgeir looks on in shock at the suggestion. "Don't you think doing one match after another is a bit too much… considering I'm now in agony because you struck me into the bookcase… doesn't seem fair… to fight me again so quickly after I was greatly injured." Atgeir replies, trying to get himself out of losing again. "Maybe we can do the rematch… tomorrow if you're even interested?" He sets forth his own suggestion so he can prepare something better.

"Whatever you say, Geir… just don't ask for another rematch so I can just you again," He says, knowing how his brother is with these things. "Like that is going to happen again. I'm improving daily, so tomorrow won't be like today, you'll see." Atgeir tries to retort back with a smug smirk.

"Enjoyed your little game, I see." They hear their father behind them, turning to him. They see him, looking over them, visibly proud of Leifur's skill. "I assume you didn't use pyromancy, in case it could have missed and burned all the book to ash." Eilif says, hoping for a correct response.

With his head lowered, Leifur replies. "Right… that was why I didn't… use it… Father." Getting a smile and a nod from his father. "Good, now come with me. It's time for today's training." Eilif puts his hand on Leifur's shoulder. "Right, father." He says, going along with Eilif out of the library, leaving Atgeir alone, standing there with a part of him angry that his brother is getting personal training from their father.

He hears the sound of two people giggling on the other side of the bookcase. "Aada, I know you are there; come out." Atgeir orders them out in a rude tone. Slowly, she comes around the bookcase to him, still giggling. He looks at her coldly, changing his expression as he sees who is with her behind that bookcase. Revna. She walks behind his sister with her beautiful pinkish blonde hair tight in a bun, her honey-brown eyes, and her fair complexion. She wears an intricate light turquoise and white dress. "Nice to see you, Atgeir." Revna says in a warm, friendly manner.

Atgeir looks slightly away, not wanting them to see the blush on his face. Closing his eyes momentarily, he turns his face back to them, leaning against the bookcase. "It's nice to see you too, Revna. Didn't think you'd come over today." He says, trying to act confident around her.

"Are you glad that I came then?" Revna says teasingly, making it harder for Atgeir to keep it together. He responds to this by mostly keeping his confident tone. "It is always a pleasure…. to have you come visit."

Aada holds her hand to her mouth, trying not to laugh at her brother's words. She doesn't want to make anyone feel bad. "Do you have any thoughts on what we can do for fun this lovely day?" She asks him, holding one of her hands to her hip with a cheeky smirk.

"Of course… I have something in mind; we can… we can go outside and play in the garden, skip some stones across the pond… see which stone goes the furthest." Atgeir says, having thought of it in a hurry. "That sounds like it could lead to something enjoyable to do later… you coming, Aada?" Revna says, asking Aada to come along.

Cheerfully, she nods. "Yes, that sounds fun." Crossing her arms, she smiles over at him. "I just hope you don't cheat again, this time by using your electromancy to get the stone to go further… we are not all as far into our arcane training." Revna teasingly comments. "Of course not, I would never do such a thing… again." Atgeir says with a courteous bow, crossing his fingers behind his back, intent to cheat a little to impress her. "Sure…. let's go then." Revna says, sounding a bit hesitant.

She takes Aada's hand as they all run off to the garden for something to do while Leifur is busy training. They do not notice Thyra looking at all this happening from a hiding place behind a table, as she is not supposed to be seen by anyone from outside the palace because of her curse.

Waking up as the sun's rays shine across his face through the cracked window, he gets up slowly and moves over to take his coat from the table next to the bed. Getting up, he puts it on and then the backpack, trying to get that dream he had of his childhood out of his head.

He looks down from the second floor where this room is, watching the villagers go about with their day, starting to reconstruct their homes. Far to the side, he can see Kamaria and Fritz waiting at the horses at the village's stables, with Kaylan peering from behind a large pile of hay.

They are ready to go - that's perfect, he ponders as he goes down and out of the partially bashed-in building.

Standing beside her horse, Kamaria slyly peaks behind her at Kaylan hiding away. "Something bothering you?" She asks him. "It's nothing just… not in the… talking with other people mood." He answers while trying to keep his voice down. Kamaria just rolls her eyes at him, looking ahead. "You've gotten into quite the anti-social mood than from the fort to here, Kay. What's the matter, pal?" Fritz comments jokingly as he leans over on the stable to get a better look at Kaylan.

"I think I will go ahead… maybe see Master Glynn and say we are coming his way." He says meekly, getting a slight smile from Kamaria. "Uh…. sure thing, we will see you there." She says, uncertain in her tone.

"Thanks." Kaylan says, shape-shifting into his horse form. He gallops off in a burst of speed.

"You really going to let him go without going through some long list of questions like you always do on things like this, like why he's like that now?" Fritz asks her, unsure of her motive. "I am certain he will tell me in his own good time. I know him. We were friends for years, and besides, such things need to be handled with more finesse than bluntness." She tells him that she is highly assured of her stance.

"All well and good by me; I'd rather not over-think such things - hurts the old head." Fritz taps against his head. "Oh, Kam…. Andy is coming this way." He points past her to Atgeir, walking toward them.

"Prince Atgeir, you're here. Ready to head off?" Kamaria asks as she mounts her horse. Atgeir gets on a horse as well. "You ain't a bit curious why our little puca friend isn't here?" Fritz asks as he prances past him on his horse. Atgeir just says in a rudely uninterested way, "Not in the slightest." Kamaria looks at him, unfazed by his reaction, as she has already figured him out. "Rude, ain't he?" Fritz whispers to her. "Kam, you think we should go now? Everyone's here and ready?" He says, laying over his horse's head, looking back in a laid-back fashion to Kamaria. She gives a nod, making Fritz yell out enthusiastically. "Great.... full speed ahead, bud!" Fritz says, galloping off with his horse. Atgeir gives a sigh as he follows him.

"This is only going to get more and more interesting." Kamaria says to herself, ready to follow.

"Wait !" She halts as she hears someone cry out to her. An old man with a large mane of grey hair runs up to her. "Is there anything wrong, sir ?" She asks him concerned. "Yes… Maybe… My name is Ronan Lynch, and I just want to know if you are with that white-furred puca; I wanted to talk to him, but he seemed to have vanished." He replies, desperate to find him.

"You mean Kaylan; yes, I know him."

"Yes, that is his name; I just want you to ask him why he and his friend just left our village… he couldn't have been responsible for what happened that night… please tell him to come back." Ronan elaborates his request in full, clenching his old hands together.

"Don't fret, I will tell him for you." She tells him with a warm smile. "Thank you. He is the only family I have left," he says, keeping himself from tearing up as he walks away weakly.

She watches him leave, filled with new questions. What happened to you, Kaylan? She ponders as she rides off with more and more unanswered questions than answers to them. She will solve each and every one of them; there is nothing out there that can't be solved and discovered.

CHAPTER 15
Hurdle in our path

Blair teleports after them at a fair distance, with Dark holding tightly onto her. She didn't get much sleep, so she struggles with creating each portal as she goes through them to make the next, then the next, as one's mana only naturally regenerates during rest.

As she pushes herself forward to create another portal, she feels light-headed. It fails to open, leaving her tumbling onto the ground as she tried to jump through the portal that wasn't there.

Blaire lays flat in the dirt. She gets up shakily, hearing Dark hissing at her. "What's your problem? I can't help it. You kept me up most of the night !…. I don't have much mana left, you…." She shouts at him, silencing up as she hears Kamaria's voice in the distance.

Sneakily, she crawls over to the top of the hill ahead of her, looking through the grass to see that she is standing further down, facing terror beasts with the other two. That's fortunate for Blaire; at least she can rest a moment now. She sighs in relief at the thought as she plops down to take a moment to get her breath.

A gigantic salamander-like terror beast stands before them on its hind legs, along with four smaller scaly, felines-like bat-eared, saber-toothed beasts. Atgeir, Kamaria, and Fritz all watch on, ready to strike. Their horses have run away.

One of the saber-toothed beasts lunges out at Fritz, who quickly sidesteps it while conjuring a mace in his hand to bash it, sending it flying to Kamaria. "Kam, look out!" He yells out to her. Kamaria creates a shard of yellow light in the air, shooting right through it. "Got it !" She shouts cheerfully as Atgeir dashes beneath this towards the most immense terror beast, slashing at it with an electrified jab aimed at its throat. It slams its claws down, almost getting Atgeir.

Fritz grabs him back by his collar, saving him from being crushed. Atgeir shoves Fritz away out of anger for touching him and interfering when not asked as he returns to fighting the salamander terror beast. Fritz just shrugs it off, returning to fighting a saber-toothed beast, still slightly annoyed at what he did.

While another one of the saber-toothed beasts comes at her from the side. She manifests a flower-shaped light shield in front of her, blocking its needle-like claws. The beast bashes at it with its spiked tail, breaking it to pieces. She leaps back, creating four light shards she sends into the beast, slaying another.

As Fritz rolls out of the way of an attacking saber-toothed beast, he tries to slash at it with a sword. Unable to keep up with its attack, he tries to block with the sword, but it swipes it out of his hand, sending it falling away. Quickly, Fritz conjures two crossbows, shooting the one in front of him point-blank in the head, then shooting another one that's charging at him to his side in the chest, slaying all of them.

Atgeir leaps back at the swipe from the giant beast's massive claws. Jumping on top of it, he kicks the beast in the head, his boot enveloped in crimson lighting, shocking it in a daze as it gets hit back.

Dashing in to slice its neck with its electrified clawed gauntlets, the beast snaps out of its daze, one of its claws swiping down at Atgeir. The swipe is stopped by Kamaria shooting a light shard into one of its eyes and Fritz shooting out the other with his crossbow, making it reel back in pain. Allowing Atgeir to finish it off as he scratches across its throat, sending a wave of scarlet electricity slashing across it, slaying it.

It falls down with a loud thud, ending this deadly encounter.

Atgeir sits down to clean himself from the fight, fixing his collar up from being pulled on and stroking back his hair in vanity. Fritz walks over to Kamaria, a fair bit away from him. "That was kinda fun, Kam. Except for Atgy being ungrateful, but that's expected by now from that royal pain… can't we just ditch him? We know what we have to do now. We don't really need him." Fritz says, still a bit annoyed.

"He surely is, but we did give our word to assist him. Both Kaylan and I will always keep our word." She reminds him, getting a strained smile from Fritz. "Okay, I'll keep going along with it… only and only because I consider you a friend." He says, holding one finger up to her, emphasizing his point.

"That's kind of you…. one thing though, can you go find and bring the horses back?" She says cheerfully, adding a request for him.

Fritz cocks his head. "Yeah, sure, I'll get right to it." He says as he spins around, giving a playful salute before he strides off.

High above them, an insectoid-looking terror beast flies, having observed the entire fight against the terror beasts below.

It flies off quickly, far away across lakes, forests, and fields, until it goes up a mountain near Astera Bay. Way up to a cave at the very top, where it enters. The blood chimera sits in the middle of this cave, the walls covered with clusters of crystals of different colors, resting on its side with its wings wrapped around it.

The small insect terror beast lands in front of the chimera. Its eyes start to light, changing to a blur of different colors. Giving forth a message the chimera can distinguish. "They are coming…. my way then… good…... will these be worth fighting…." It says in its broken manner, tapping its claws against the stone floor.

"Better make better, stronger monsters…… to go and fight… them when they….. arrive at the city…. below." He starts laughing wickedly, slamming his fist down on the insect beast. Crushing it flat, he picks it up with the other clawed hand. "I Apologize, my flying creation…. needs more material for….. better creations." It says, getting up to walk over to a horrendous pile of dead animals, dirt, branches, plants, and rocks.

The chimera sits down next to it, starting to form more powerful terror beasts from it, keeping a crazed grin spread on its face the entire time.

CHAPTER 16
Welcome to Astera Bay

In the Severne realm, inside the Hyvits palace.

The evening light shines through the three large golden framed windows of the study with bookcases made of entirely white fir wood along two sides of the room, on top of a glistening obsidian stone floor. In the center of this room, sitting behind an ebony desk with a golden vine pattern on the sides and the Solstris family crest carved onto the front of it. Eilif sits at this desk, wearing his crown - made of silver and gold- to resemble fines meeting in the center with a pair of wings going off to the sides and a yellow diamond embedded in the center.

He is busy reading over two reports on Sulfrens sent to him by his scouts at the Myrsna mountain range and along the outskirts of the realm. The Crows stand by, watching him intently from the other side of the room.

The first report came from the outskirts:

Your Highness.

This is an urgent matter to attend to - a pack of seven lesser Sulfrens has been spotted prowling near the mountainous village of Tolumi. Coming out at night, they make their way into the town. Snatching up the inhabitants from their houses. I have failed to prevent their attempts, as the Sulfrens are far too fast for me to catch. I followed them up the mountainside, south of the village, losing them among the crags. I am unable to find where the Sulfren pack is hidden. I suspect they could be Within the vast cave network underneath that area, yet I had no luck finding them there.

If this continues, the entire village will be gone in a matter of days.

Having finished reading it, Eilif puts it down to one side. Sounds drastic. Still, there is one more sulfren report to go through:

Your Highness, this is a letter of great importance.

A grand Sulfren has been spotted, slowly making its way across the Far Grelu Plains, leaving a trail of destruction in its path. The sulfren stands in size comparison, roughly larger than a full-grown Alder tree. Its entire body is covered in a dense bone-like armor that's tougher than steel. Unwavering in its intent on walking a straight course, crushing anything in its way. Our scouting party attempted to face the threat, yet our efforts were in vain. Our attacks couldn't even scratch the monster's thick armor. It has already

Eilif finishes reading and places it on top of the previous one. Sitting back
in his seat, he goes into thought, going over what he has to do next. This
one is an intimidating situation, a titan sulfren of the juggernaut variant. It's
quite powerful.... still, it won't need his personal assistance in dealing with
it.

"Nerium !" Eilif calls out to the Crow. Catching her attention, Nerium
rushes over to him, kneeling in front of the desk, instinctively feeling
anxious about why he asked for her. "I need you to go and take a tracking
party up to the Myrsna mountain range to locate and slay a pack of Sulfrens
in the cave network near Tolumi. Is that clear, Nerium?" Eilif orders her.
Nerium stands back up, giving a slight bow. "Of course, your Highness. I'll
do it right away." She chirps before sprinting out of the room. She is excited
to head out without the other Crows or even the king, with the opportunity
to investigate the Sulfrens after she completes the mission. "Wolfsbane,
Larkspur !" Eilif calls out to them. Turning his head towards the king,
Wolfsbane obediently walks up to the desk with Larkspur. "What do you
require, your Highness." He asks, kneeling down before him with the other
Crow alongside him. "You will have to cooperate with Larkspur to slay a
grand Sulfren on its way from the east towards Reterius. Teleport is over
there at once; there is no saying how long the monster will take to reach that
town." Eilif commands them.

Getting up to his feet, Wolfsbane nods. "As you say, your Highness." He
answers him respectfully, holding onto Larkspur's hand. Both vanish in a
white flash of light and teleported to their destination. Leaving Eilif with
the last remaining Crow there. "Nightshade, you'll be on standby for now

until I have need of you." Eilif says, looking over at the Crow silently standing against the wall with his arms crossed. Nightshade gives a bow before leaving the room to stand outside the closed door. Guarding it intently, close by as he awaits any task King Eilif would call him for. Now left alone, Eilif looks over the mountain of papers stacked on his right concerning different aspects of the realm he has to look over. This is going to take some time to finish, Eilif reckons. Giving a sigh, he takes one from the pile. It will be tedious, but still, it has to be done, and he'd rather have it be himself doing it, approving and going over every detail in these papers in an absolutely correct fashion.

Suddenly, a thought pops into his mind: about how well Leifur would have done with this part of being king, its far less exciting parts. No, it doesn't matter; he's gone forever. There is no use in thinking of the past and what could have been; all he can do now is control what happens in the present and the future with Atgeir as his successor, who'll return from his punishment to the Abyss defense tower better than he ever left. Eilif is certain. This will just be another long day of work, not unlike any other; this one will just be one of the more tedious than others.

Somewhere in another area of the Hyvits palace....

Thyra watches her mother and Aada with one of the Crows, Nightshade, who is standing by their side. She observes them from a distance in the palace's training room, which is filled with racks of weapons, an adorned metal chest with various items that are needed for each session, and wooden combat practice dummies. Seeing her sister being taught further in her healing magic, specifically the moonlight healing variant, she is now ready for this advanced form.

Between Sia and Aada lies a carmine-red semi-translucent dummy with a sizeable deep slice across its chest and strange inky black symbols spreading from across the body. Holding up her hand, Sia swishes it to and fro, creating a pale silver orb of swirling lights, which she gently places on the gash. It expands, slowly dissipating in a shimmer with the wounds closing up, and the malicious-looking symbols disappear entirely.

"That's how it's done; this spell will heal the most horrid of wounds, as well as almost any curse. Remember to keep the flow of mana on the orb and in it, swirling across it in a controlled flowing manner," Sia explains to her daughter, who is listening intently.

"Can I give it another try now, mother?" Aada asks politely.

"Of course, Aada, let's see how well you do on your first attempt." Sia says warmly. Gesturing to Nightshade to come. Both of them get up to stand away from the body. As Nightshade unsheathes a sword made of black steel with a black start sapphire at the hilt's end. A strange purple energy envelops the weapon as he slices down at it. It leaves a horrible deep gash with the same inky patterns as before.

Aada crouches down as she does the same gesture her mother did, creating the silver orb of mana. It looks fine at first, but as she places it closer, the swirls become more extensive and more chaotic as it fizzles out in an impressive flurry of little lights. Aada looks at her failure sadly. "I almost got it right." She says meekly.

Crouching beside her: "Let's try that again, my dear." Her mother says, motivating her. Aada makes another silver orb, focusing intensely on doing it now, not noticing her mother looking off to the distance, her mind wandering off again.

Still watching from afar, wondering when she will tell her father about Atgeir. Thyra thinks as she leaves the room to stand around in the hallway. She is no longer interested in looking at Aada and getting the love and caring attention she craves dearly, but she is confident that will all change in time. Where Atgeir is now and what he is doing doesn't matter; if he succeeds, she gets something, and if he fails, as well.

Along the busy harbor of Astera Bay on this cloudy day, fish are being sold along the street, and the city's denizens go about their daily work in this seaside city. Kamaria, Atgeir, and Fritz walk along in a group through this crowded street. Atgeir stares at everyone as he goes along with Kamaria. "So this is the realm's second biggest city. I only saw parts of the biggest, Celandinia. When I visited your realm's royal family a hundred and twelve years ago when I was still a child. Still nothing as impressive as the cities of my realm." Atgeir says with a tone of superiority to Kamaria and Fritz.

"Would be great to go to the Severne realm to actually see it; it would be nice to have another realm to compare how things differentiate, like buildings, wildlife, and uses of magic." Kamaria speaks her thoughts out loud.

"I, for one, wouldn't be able to tell for myself how great a should city look, considering I'm not some hundreds of years old elf royal and brilliant lady; in my opinion, everywhere looks ten times better because of where I grew up." Fritz comments in a laid-back manner, adding his opinion on the matter for the very sake of it.

"Like any of you can come to my realm. I suspect a traveler's stone isn't in any of your price range." Atgeir says, still in a mocking tone. "I did have one when I came to this realm but lost it years back. You could be generous and take us with you when you're done to see." Kamaria replies. "No, I'm not; it wasn't in the deal. You can try coming when you use the reward I give you for your assistance." He says bluntly.

"I guess so, I shouldn't have asked then." She says, placing a finger on her chin. "Fritz, do you want to come along when Kaylan and I go to the Severne realm one day? I think you'd like seeing how different it looks there; it might be fun." She asks him.

"Maybe; it depends on what I feel like doing then," Fritz answers as they approach a very odd-looking building with multiple metal pipes going about it. This three-floor tall building is made of mismatched bricks of numerous colors, with windows in different shapes and sizes and a couple of chimneys above emanating a strange pink smoke.

"I will look forward to your answer then," Kamaria says as she walks up to the door covered in paintings of a herd of prancing deer. Kamaria knocks on it, waiting for someone to come and open it up, but no one comes.

"Maybe he's out!....." Fritz says, jumping in fright as he hears someone tap his back and a burst of air behind him.

They all turn around to see a man with ginger hair with a grey streak through it and emerald green eyes with one covered by an eyepatch, wearing an oversized red robe-like coat adorned with magenta swirling patterns across it, hanging from his slim figure. "Welcome, welcome Kamaria and…. associates." He says, giving a dramatic bow while holding onto a staff made of copper with a pezzottaite gem on the top of it.

"Master Glynn, it's so nice to see you again." Kamaria rushes in for a big hug. "Nice to see you too." He says as she lets go of him so he can talk to the others. "Oh….. let me introduce myself, I am Master Oran Glynn. High sorcerer in the Thiar realm's arcane court, proficient telekinetics, telepathy, and summoning." He says courteously to Fritz and Atgeir.

He goes over to Fritz first, giving him a hearty handshake. "You must be the laid-back but always entertaining jokester, Fritz." He says, getting a cheeky reply in return. "I do try my best to keep things lively." Oran then goes to Atgeir, trying to take his hand to shake, but Atgeir just pulls it away, glaring at him coldly. "Prince Atgeir Solstris, I presume. Come to help defeat this menace threatening us but cutting off the root of the problem, the Blood chimera." He says, giving an awkward little bow with a wide grin.

"The puca creature told you about me and the whole situation then… did you figure out the exact location of the chimera in the area," Atgeir asks, getting straight to the point. "Yes, Kaylan did. We can discuss it inside, though." Oran suggests.

"Perfect, it's far better than being outside here with the smell." Atgeir says, looking back at all the stalls heaps selling fish.

"Come on in then; I'll get some tea and some oatcakes while we converse and some coffee, especially to your taste, dear Kamaria." He says as he opens the door, going through with Atgeir.

Fritz stays put, looking to the side. "Aren't you coming in?" Kamaria asks as she waits at the door, noticing this. "I'm just gonna explore the city a bit; you don't really need me around for this part, Kam." He replies, holding his hands to his waist. "Certainly, just a little suggestion, though. You should check out the Merry Pelican; I walked past it several times. It seems like a place you'll quite enjoy getting a drink and a meal in. You need to eat something after the long ride here." She says, waving.

"I'll look out for it; it sounds amazing." Fritz replies, closely watching her as she enters the building, closing the door behind her.

Blaire watches Fritz come from behind a barrel in an alley. "You're here, B. Knew you'd come along anyway, even with Kam saying you shouldn't!" He shouts out, glad to see her. Blaire gets up, with Dark still clinging tightly to her back.

"And what is that thing?" He says, walking behind her. Looking up and down the little monster's body, trying to figure out what this thing even is. "It kind of followed me and ended up latching onto me. Now I can't really get it off." Blaire says in a quite tired and defeated tone. Fritz looks up to her, crouched low. He starts to snicker a bit at her situation. "It isn't funny, you dolt !" She yells, making him laugh even more.

"Yea… Yea." He says, catching his breath from all the laughing. He holds his hand to his chest as he gets up, seeing Blaire look at him angrily. "Alright, let me try then to take the thing off; you do tend to give.." He grabs it, beginning to pull on it, but it still holds on. "… too easily." He puts his foot up against her back, trying to get more leverage as he pulls on it harder, but it still holds on. Putting his other foot to her back to try to get more leverage, they end up both tumbling backward. Falling to the ground with Dark still holding on firmly.

Fritz rolls away on his back. Holding onto his head, he grins widely. "That thing's holding on for dear life; it's practically glued to you." He says, getting up. "Looks like you're gonna have to get used to living with it." Fritz says jokingly.

Getting a disappointed look from Blair. "Cheer up; I think there might be something to cheer you up." He says, holding his hand to her.

She grabs hold of it, Fritz pulling her up to her feet. "Kam, just told me of this place we can get some drinks and a nice meal…. you in?" He says with a cheerful smile.

"That sounds nice." She agrees.

Fritz quickly rushes over to a crate with a piece of sailcloth hanging over it, snatching it up to bring over to her.

"I think you just have to wear this over that thing on your back - it keeps people from staring." He suggests. Taking it, she does just that. "Thanks, I guess." She replies, a bit unsure of it but happy to go and get something to eat.

CHAPTER 17
The terror beasts attack

Sitting in the building's living room are Oran, Kamaria, Kaylan, and Atgeir around a low wooden table with a wave design on the sides of it. The room is filled with shelves of trinkets and odd ends, like an assortment of crystals and vials of glowing liquids, a unicorn horn, a plate of strange gold coins with a clover symbol on each, a small silver harp, and fairy wings.

Around them fly tiny hummingbirds made of bronze, zooming about to different sections of the house with small glowing trails of color following each.

"There has been talk of strange noises, growling, and screeching coming from around the mountain further west of the city, mostly at night. I summoned my four nature spirits to look around the area." Oran tells them, taking a sip from his tea before continuing on. "But they didn't return for days, so I tried to summon them again. Only for them to reappear as chard corpses."

"That's horrible!..... I remember them being so kind during our training matches.... could you at least figure something out... from their bodies on what we're going up against." She asks, genuinely sad about the loss of the spirits, but her intellectual mind wants to know as much as possible about what did this. Kaylan is stunned by this but is always interested in learning more about the threat. "Actually, I did find something on it; the lingering mana on them felt otherworldly, like something I have never felt in my entire life of studying magic, something ancient." He explains that he is not quite sure how to describe it.

"Sounds similar to the descriptions my father felt as he fought against the divines in the war; he told me one night of this." Atgeir chips in with the answer.

Oran's face lights up at these words. "Traces that are similar to that of a divine, interesting. They shouldn't be able to do anything; they were stripped of all their mana and the ability to regenerate it back." He says, trying to think of something.

"This chimera could be a remnant of the divine, one that survived getting its arcane powers stolen; there can't be any other way." Kaylan speaks up, trying to give his own explanation.

Kamaria is opposed to this statement. "That can't be right; Valo Munari's spell went after their higher mana signatures themselves; none of them could have hidden from it." She points out.

"That's right, that spell was created by my grandfather from my mother's side, but still of a great noble lineage. They are revered highly in our realm for their skill and power. His spell wouldn't allow any of them to escape its reach." Atgeir strangely agrees with Kamaria.

Kaylan looks on with shock. "Those are good points and all, but what other reason is there? do you have any thoughts on it, Master Glynn ?" The young puca asks him. Oran thinks for a bit, resting his head on his hand. "We won't know for certain till we can examine the chimera's body." He says, getting up to his feet with a confident look about him. "We just need to slay it and bring it back…. this is why I talked to King Eoghan to form the Arcana regiment to defeat it and learn about this threat. Instead of just sending his uninformed men, let's show those monsters our might." He says enthusiastically.

"Well said." Kamaria shouts out, sharing his enthusiasm.

"All of us just need to go to the mountain and….." Oran stumbles back with his last word as everything shakes violently around, making everything on the shelves fall off, as they hear a tremendously loud sound.

Crash!!!!

From the distance, a loud sound reaches them.

Regaining his balance, Oran rushes to the window, peering at a massive plume of black smoke rising further away between wrecked buildings. The sound of screaming is heard, along with ferocious screeches and roars. "They came to us, that saves the trip to the mountain… perfect." He says with a big grin as he notices a pair of crimson wings within the rising smoke and dust.

Fritz and Blaire leap out of the burning building that was the Merry Pelican, each holding a couple of people.

Running away past the wooden sign of the establishment that used to depict a pelican resting on an anchor, now broken on the floor. They dash behind a building a decent distance away that is more intact, away from the dust and falling debris around them. They place everyone they saved carefully on the ground. Looking back in horror, they can see the blood chimera flying up above, higher - with each flap of its wings, a powerful gust of wind blows loose debris across the city street.

Dark lets loose of Blaire, leaping off of her. He runs away on all four, vanishing inside a hole in the wall. "Now it…. stinking let's go. That blasted little monster kept me up all night!" Blaire yells out furiously, gesturing angrily at him.

"This is not the time for that, B. We've got company, right there!" Fritz says shakily, grabbing her chin to point it towards a terror beast looking at them from the building's corner. It is an intimidating-looking beast. It was a giant, thin, gangly, humanoid bat with patches of green fur across its grey body and two long, spindly, metal-clawed arms in front of its torn wings. Its four large, completely red eyes locked onto Fritz and Blaire.

Fritz quickly conjures a sword; without a thought he dashes off forward, swiftly getting past it, dodging a sonic scream from the beast while making a slash across one of its legs. "Keep them safe, I'm leading this thing away!" He yells out to Blaire, running away with the bat beast, screeching wildly in pursuit of him.

She looks back at the unconscious people before looking around nervously for any other terror beasts.

She overlooks the black and green striped eel-like terror beast slithering down from above, with orange glowing tendrils moving across its body as it comes closer and closer to her.

Bounding across rooftops, Atgeir, Kamaria, and Kaylan rush hastily toward where the terror beasts are, with Oran levitating along with them. "We're almost on them…. keep your wits about you; this bunch feels a lot…." Oran says, stopping in the air as a spiked lizard-like terror beast pounces up from below, slamming into Oran.

The collision sent both him and the beast crashing to the ground.

Kamaria peers back for a moment, but only for a moment, as she is confident her master doesn't need her to go back and help him. She keeps going until both of them reach the crater in the middle of the destroyed area where the blood chimera is above all this destruction.

The chimera notices their presence; it gestures with its claw, pointing to both Kaylan and Kamaria. Sending a lightning-fast pitch-black weasel-like terror beast with two glowing red eyes. It follows her as she runs off, countering it by shooting light shards at the beast, leaving the area in haste to escape its speedy barrage of strikes.

A giant chameleon-like terror beast appears on the building next to them, shooting out a glowing purple tongue. Wrapping around a frightened Kaylan, it runs away with him. Dragging Kaylan along, screaming, away from the area.

"Now it… it is just us…. show me your power…. Elf!" The chimera yells, grinning ferociously. "You'll regret that, monster!" Atgeir yells back and leaps at the chimera with a burst of scarlet lighting, ready with both of his gauntlets enveloped in electricity. Slashing at him in mid-air at his chest. The chimera avoids it easily, moving his body slightly to the side. Atgeir keeps momentum, hitting the building behind the chimera; he pushes back on the wall, shattering the window nearby. In a shock wave, he leaps forward for another attack. The chimera dodges him again, but when he gets past him this time, his tail lashes downward on Atgeir's back, sending him shooting down to the ground in a crash.

He looks up slowly to see the chimera flying down to land next to him. "Is this…. all you can do, elf." He sneers, angering Atgeir.

"That's just the warm-up, monster." Atgeir retorts.

CHAPTER 18
A horrible outcome

Kamaria stands shakily, her clothes torn, with cuts all over her body. Her eyes are tracking the weasel terror beast as it runs all around her at blinding speeds, bouncing across the building's walls. She creates her shield of light, and at the last second, it lunges at her, knocking her back a few meters as it hits the shield, breaking it in a burst of thousands of little lights.

Kamaria rolls out of the way, missing a blow just a little as it charges at her. This thing is going so fast that she can't think up her next move quickly enough; she realizes she is stumbling about tiredly. Her mana is mostly depleted; she creates a couple of light shards, shooting them at the beast. The terror beast dogged almost everyone, with one just making a small cut on its face. It snarls wildly. It charged at her and slashed her with both clawed paws in a barrage of strikes across her body.

It stands back as she collapses to the ground, looking on in victory.

She was scared that this might be the end, scared that the life she had set forth of discovering and learning everything there was in the known realms and beyond could be cut short.

Being lunged head first through a brick wall by the force of the bat beast's sonic screech, Fritz lands with a skid into the side of a dining table, screaming out in pain. Fritz flops about trying to get up, as his arms give way every time he tries to push himself up.

The bat terror beast enters through the hole, relishing in its prey, who is struggling to get back to his feet.

Fritz conjures a crossbow, holding it weakly to the beast. He pulls back the trigger, shooting the arrow through its ear instead of the creature's head he was aiming at.

Fritz slams his fist to the ground, frustrated. Surrounded by bricks, broken glass, and wood, he looks on as it approaches him, its fanged mouth agape.

Biting himself loose from the chameleon beast's tongue, giving off a flash of light and the headache for doing it, now in wolf form. Kaylan falls down behind the creature, rolling painfully to a stop on a roof. The terror beast stops in its tracks, retracting its injured tongue. Hastily, Kaylan uses his telekinetic power to launch the mind orb to it, seeing the flash of light with the headache again as he feels the sensation of wind spiraling across him.

The impact of the attack does no damage as it hits the beast. Looking scared, he quickly shapeshifts into his raven form, trying to fly away, only to be knocked out of the air by the chameleon beast tongue. He plummets down to the ground, reverting back to his human form. The beast leaps down behind him, falling straight on top of him and knocking Kaylan unconscious from the mighty blow.

Atgeir runs up to it, and as he jumps up, he kicks upward with an arc of red lighting; the chimera blocks the kick by grabbing onto his leg. He swings Atgeir around, throwing him away from him.

Atgeir lands on his feat hastily and starts running around to the chimera; going faster, his body envelopes in scarlet electricity as he flies around in what appears as balls of lighting shooting around the chimera, looking like a ring of electricity.

Atgeir charges out of it, coming from the chimera's back. He comes to a halt as he whips the electricity off the clawed tips of his gauntlets, sending ten strips of lightning shooting toward it. The chimera looks back momentarily, noticing this. It violently spreads its wings, creating a powerful gust of wind. Sending the attack back at him, Atgeir hastily falls flat on the floor as it breaks the building wall behind him. His attacks are doing nothing to the chimera. Desperate, he decides to use the Volt Star - he still can't use it correctly, but he has no choice.

Jumping up, he runs at the chimera with one of his hands in a fist covered in electricity. He tries to punch him again, and like before, he dodges it. Now behind him, Atgeir leaps onto his back. Grabbing tightly onto him with one of his arms and legs, he uses his free hand to form the volt star. The chimera screeches angrily at him as Atgeir hastily shoves the ball of lightning into its mouth. "Die, you vile creature!" Atgeir yells out.

It blows up in a powerful explosion, sending Atgeir flying backward off of it.

He gets up in a daze, looking around him in a cloud of dust. Barely able to see anything before him, he looks ahead, trying to see where the chimera is. Grinning smugly, he gets to his feet. "And that is that." Atgeir says, clapping his hands together and laughing happily that he beat that monster.

A bright orange glow starts to emanate from the thick cloud of dust, along with blue sparks of lightning arcing from it. "Now that is better…. nice and strong." He hears the broken voice of the chimera as it walks into his view. Atgeir eyes are filled with complete and utter fear he hasn't experienced in more than a century…. but he has genuinely never faced something that fights so viciously and maliciously in his entire life. Looking at its face, having a small gash coming from its mouth to its left ear. Atgeir backs up quickly, trying to run away, but the chimera just leaps over him, blocking his path. "Where are you going, elf…. the fun is just beginning." The chimera says as he claws at Atgeir a couple of times on the chest, and with the final blow, he kicks him across the crater. The creature's mind now filled with a mad frenzy.

"Come on, fight back…." The chimera says, looking at the injured elf trying to walk weakly away, holding onto his deep wounds.

With a burst of speed, the chimera flies to him, slamming him down to the ground with Atgeir clenching both of his fists at…. his sides as the pain courses through his body. It backs off, ready for another attack with its claws.

Atgeir closes his eyes for the next blow.

But nothing happens…

…Absolutely nothing………

Opening his eyes weakly. The first thing he sees is an orange and brown cloak in front of him, waving in the breeze…… looking slowly up, he is met by his brother's face with the chimera standing further away, bearing its sharp fangs. "Leifur…." Atgeir says as he passes out from the blood loss.

"Do you really want to end this now? You seem like the monster that would enjoy facing his opponent at its strongest... one that enjoys the fight." Leifur says, directed at the chimera. "What… do you mean…. elf." It asks, frustrated that Leifur stopped him. "Just give me ten days, and he'll be trained up enough to give you a really worthy fight." Leifur suggests keeping a calm demeanor. The creature stands there in thought, holding his gaze fixed on him. "Why don't you fight me now…. you look strong." The chimera says, smiling wickedly.

"It's not my fight; Geir started this fight, so it's his to finish. I won't just take that from him… if you try to go after me, I'll just leave, and you won't be able to catch me; I'm certain of that. Depriving you of a worthwhile battle." Leifur explains his reasoning to the savage monster. The chimera's smile becomes bigger at this, laughing wildly. "Fine….. have your time… I will be waiting… at the base of the…. mountain west of this… place of rock structures." It says before he lets out a deafening roar, signaling his terror beasts to come to him immediately.

The chimera takes to the sky with a burst of speed. As the terror beasts that came with him here. Returns from all corners, running across the roofs after him.

Oran Levitates above the city, holding onto an unconscious Blaire. Having slain the terror beast that attacked him. He found her lying on top of a roof, beaten and bruised. He descends down slowly, still holding onto her.

He places her down gently, holding his staff with one hand while he uses the other to draw a sign in light above the gem on the staff with his finger. Summoned out of a cloud of smoke, a dozen winged humanoid beings of ever-changing colors of light appear - they are known as luxins. "Take her to my house and heal her, find as many injured as you can, and do the same." Oran commands them. One goes over to Blaire, picks her up, and flies off. The others go off in various directions to search the city.

Leifur jumps down from the roof of the building behind Oran. Atgeir is held across his shoulder, so he walks up to him, placing Atgeir at his feet. "Here's another one for you."

"Alright, one more coming up." Oran says, shaking his head with a grin, glad Atgeir is found quickly. He does the same thing as before, summoning a luxin back. "I found one for you; go take him back as it was told before."

He says, pointing to Atgeir. The luxin does this hastily; picking him up, it flies away like the others.

CHAPTER 19
Getting back up…. from failure

Hundred and nine years ago in the Severne Realm.

Atgeir and Leifur walk around the Tidis forest at night, their path illuminated by the moon's light coming down through the foliage above and a couple of fireflies going about the forest. Atgeir follows his brother, nervously watching his surroundings intensely as he walks along slowly. Scared that a sulfren or something else might jump out of the shadows to attack them.

Feeling something on his back, Atgeir jumps back in fright. Seeing that it is only his brother who touched his back. Leifur chuckles at his reaction; Atgeir looks back at his brother madly. "That wasn't any funny, Leifur." He yells, pointing angrily at him. "Were you actually scared of that?" Leifur asks jokingly.

"Of course I am; only a fool wouldn't be with those sulfrens still out here. We're not powerful enough to face them… at least not yet." He yells at his brother. "And yet you came along anyway." Leifur says, unfazed by his brother's words. "You blackmailed me in coming along, the audacity." Atgeir responds to this, crossing his arms. "I learned that from you, little brother. I see why you enjoy doing it so much; it's still not something I'd do anymore; it feels quite bad after I did it." Leifur remarks. "Yeah, you should stop besides…. when I do it with more finesse." Atgeir says, looking as Leifur climbs up a tree to look ahead.

"Sure, I get it." Leifur says, his eyes scanning the area for what they came for. "Now, where is that Tuagus… I read it is real tough, so I might get to fight it in a brawl." He is still holding onto a branch of the tree and whispering to himself.

"Do you see?" Atgeir yells up to him impatiently.

"I'm still looking… wait….." Leifur replies as he sees something in the distance. A small feathery deer with big glowing white eyes. It prances about among the trees, leaving behind a luminescent trail of small lights like stars in the air. Leifur leaps off the tree and runs after it, and the Tuagus starts to run away from him. "I found it; quickly follow me!" Leifur yells to his brother. Atgeir hastily sprints off behind him.

Atgeir struggles to keep up with his brother's speed, struggling to run across the rough, getting over fallen trees, leaping across stones, and across a lake until his brother is out of sight.

Atgeir stops his pursuit, pacing; he stands up against a tree. Scared of every sound and slight movement around him, hearing a vicious growl from above, he looks above to see a sulfren climbing down slowly to him, its eyes glowing menacingly in the dark. Atgeir walks back slowly from it as the sulfren leaps down, growling at him. It violently charges at Atgeir to slice at him with its razor-sharp claws.

The young prince jumps out of the way, barely getting caught by it. Atgeir runs off as fast as he can, pursued by the sulfren. Going down a steep slope in the forest, he hears its snarls as it gets closer. He dares not look behind him to see how close it is to him. Atgeir's foot gets caught in a root sticking out of the ground he didn't notice in his desperate dash away from the monster. Atgeir stumbles forward, struggling as he keeps himself up and running shakily, met at the end of this steep slope by a stone wall. The base of a cliff, no doubt. Frantically, he tries to run to the side of it but gets rammed into the wall by the sulfren. Atgeir falls down, and quickly trying to get up, the sulfren swipes at his face with its claws, sending him falling backward onto his back.

Atgeir sits weakly up, placing his hand to his face and pulling his hand away. He gasps at the sight of blood on it. Looking past it, he sees the sulfren ready to pounce on him.

Leifur kicks the monster right in the jaw by leaping from out of a tree. Landing in front of it, he dodges most of the sulfrens, getting slashed a couple of times to the face and arms. Leifur strikes back, slapping his hands together, sending mighty sound waves crashing into it. Sending it reeling back in pain, Leifur rushes over to Atgeir, pulling him onto his back.

Leifur runs away, carrying his little brother away from the sulfren. "How will we explain this to mother and father when we get back with these scars? We're going to be in a lot of trouble." Atgeir asks weakly, still being carried by Leifur. "Don't worry; the only one who will get in trouble is me. I know what father will do." Leifur assures him in a weary tone, still keeping his pace.

Atgeir opens his eyes and instinctively bolts upright from where he is lying. He is no longer in the crater but in a bed! He breathes a heavy sigh of relief. Looking at his chest, he sees his torn coat and shirt were removed - revealing no wound. They must have taken him back here and healed it. His brother did come and save him, just like before. Leifur did say they would meet again at Astera Bay, so seeing him here shouldn't be much of a surprise. Observing the walls, he admires the surfaces covered in murals of fairies with wings like butterflies and purple to pinkish shining skin, flying around flowers in a bright forest clearing with squirrels, hedgehogs, and mice. Next to a wardrobe, on a chair, lays a new set of clothes folded up along with his silver gauntlets and boots.

Atgeir picks it up and quickly puts it on, going to the mirror to see how it looks on him. It is a grey leather sleeveless coat and trousers with black patches and intricate green and blue patterns decorating it, with his silver gauntlets and boots. Atgeir ties back his jet-black hair neatly, flattening down any stray strands. He suddenly gets a flash of what happened with the chimera, the fear he experienced, and how he felt so weak.

He stumbles back onto the bed, holding his head low between his hands. Most of his attacks against that thing didn't even affect it - it dodged almost all of them, and the one that did impact made only a small wound on its face.

Hearing people talking below, he raises his head. He hears his brother's voice among them. Slowly, Atgeir gets up and heads toward the door to speak to his brother, even if he doesn't feel like interacting with anyone at the moment…

"We have ten days then. Sounds like a reasonable amount of time to train to improve everyone's capabilities." Oran says, sitting back in a chair in the living room with Kamaria drinking coffee, Kaylan sitting next to her, Fritz sitting cross-legged on the ground, and Blaire and Leifur standing against the wall.

"Are you going to train this bunch up as well - that's a sound idea. The chimera still has his minions who attacked the city with him, and he might have made more… they need to be dealt with while Atgeir is busy fighting their master." Leifur replies to this, glad that their plan is now laid out.

"What is our training even going to be? All of us use different types of magic." Kaylan asks, interested in how this challenge is to be tackled. "Rest assured, I have a plan to train all of you to a level sufficient to defeat your opponents." Oran says, holding his finger up, sounding quite confident. "My apologies, Master Glynn, so when will…" Kaylan replies, stopping as he notices Atgeir at the door.

Walking in slowly, Atgeir observes them, seeing Blaire among them; he looks past her as if he isn't in the mood to argue with her about being here. He walks past her and goes up to Oran. "Right away… we're going to go out and train right away!" Atgeir says with a bitter hatred in his voice, impatiently wanting revenge on the Blood chimera. "We were actually waiting for you before we all went to the training ground." Oran says as he gets up and walks to the door. He stands there at the door. "But now, with you here, we can go." Oran adds, gesturing towards the door. One by one, everyone exits, with Atgeir keeping a close eye on his brother as they leave. Kamaria quickly runs up to Oran. "Master Glynn, Kaylan, and I know where the training grounds are. May I please stay a moment and talk something over with Kaylan? I think this will help him get better." She asks.

"Of course, Kamaria…. good luck with your talk." Oran says, placing his hand gently on her shoulder - knowing what she is trying to accomplish by this. She nods back. "Thanks, I will see you all there shortly." She says as Oran walks out, locking the door behind him. Kamaria walks back to her seat, looking at Kaylan, whose head is lowered with a face filled with dread.

"I have a message for you…. Ronan Lynch asked you to come back home." Kamaria tells him, hearing this. Kaylan turns his head away from her with his ears drooping down, grabbing onto his mind orb to try and comfort himself. "You talked to him… sorry, but I just can't…. go back there…. Especially after…." He says softly, looking down. Unable to complete his sentence. Kamaria reaches over to him, tapping him on the back. "Why won't you want to go back? What I can tell by talking to him is that he seems to really care about you; what actually happened between you? Is this why you are getting those horrible headaches every time you try to fight…." She goes over to him, looking directly into his eyes. Holding onto both of his arms firmly. Kaylan just turns away from her again, not having the will to look her in the eyes.

Letting go of him, she sits down on the floor next to him, placing her hands on her knees. "When I came here from the Kusini realm, I came in a team of five to learn about the other known realms and what kind of magic they use; we were sent to this one. I was the youngest among them, almost a teenager, but I was chosen to go because I was quite intelligent for my age. We went our separate ways to different parts of the realm." She looks over at Kaylan, seeing him quickly peek at her. "I asked many master sorcerers to take me under their wing so I could learn magic from this realm, but nobody wanted to take a foreigner from another world… I was alone and friendless in this realm, I knew so little of… until Master Glynn took me under his wing, and by becoming his apprentice, I met you. My greatest and most beloved friend… I didn't want to rush you to tell me, but for how long will you keep your past from me." Kamaria concludes, waiting for a response from him. A few moments pass, with just silence. She just sits there, not saying a single word to her….. She looks away sadly, getting up.

"Kamaria, wait…. I will tell you… I will tell you everything!" Atgeir yells out to her, holding his hands out to her. Kamaria looks back at him with a slight smile, returning to sit beside him. "I'm listening." She says happily that her friend will tell her about his past.

"Uh…. right…. it's a long story… but here I go… when I was a child, I used to live in the forest near a small village called Callunaton with my best friend Declan playing tricks on travelers going by and the villagers living nearby….. until that one day ten years ago." Kaylan says, starting his tale.

CHAPTER 20
Kaylan's tale

With the light of the setting sun, a young Kaylan watches from behind shrubbery and foliage hidden well in the forest with Declan, a puca with ears like that of a rabbit with multiple earrings on them, on top of his wild black hair, wearing a patched up old blue tunic, fixed up with different colors and kinds of fabrics. Declan observes the road closely with his sharp golden-hued eyes, swishing his bushy tail back and forth with excitement for their next mischievous hijinks.

Both of their ears perk up, hearing the sound of horses pulling a wagon further up the road. They look at each other, knowing what to do next as they have done this many times before.

Declan's shape shifts into the form of a pitch-black horse. Running out from where they were hiding to right in front of the wagon as it came round the bend, startling the men riding it and making the older man pull back on the reins. Their horse comes to an abrupt stop. The older man gets off the carriage, walking up to Declan in horse form. "Why do you think it just ran…. up in front of us like that, father?" The young man asks.

"Not sure; it must have escaped its stable; it doesn't have a saddle or anything on." The father says, examining the horse.

Kaylan comes out of the forest from the back and sneakily makes his way behind the wagon. He climbs into it; the wagon is filled with creates and bags. Kaylan takes a strange object from a pouch strapped to his belt, created by him but named the explosive surprise by Declan; it will be set off by the wagon's movement. It is a green pulse crystal wrapped with strange black vines with symbols drawn on with mana-imbued green paint. He opens one of the bags to place the object in it, surprised to see spell books and scrolls and a small case containing ingredients to make potions. He looks on at it with amazement. The usual people who come round here don't carry such things.

"What are you doing back there ?!" The young man yells out to Kaylan. He lets out a frightened yelp, tossing the explosive object in the air. As it lands on the wagon's floor, it goes off with a bang.

An explosive blast of green smoke and crystal shards shoot at all angles.

Declan looks back in shock at their plan backfiring. He shapeshifts back into his more human-like form, running towards the wagon to look for Kaylan. The older man looks on in fright at the explosion and Declan changing, who had just transformed from a horse to this humanoid form!

Declan jumps onto the wagon to come help. Kaylan is being held down by the young man. "Let go of him !" Declan yells, shape-shifting into a fierce, pitch-black wolf. He tackles the young man off his friend. They both tumble off the wagon. Kaylan rushes to the side, looking down at them fighting. The young man holds back his attacker by the neck as Declan tries biting at him viciously.

"Stop… Conor…. pucas stop the fighting… there is no reason for this!" The older man shouts out to all of them, now standing on top of the wagon.

With these words, everyone looks back at him in shock and disbelief. Declan shape shifts back, getting off of Conor. He climbs up the wagon next to Kaylan. "Why, Father, why don't we just fight off these scoundrels ?" He asks the older man, clearly upset at this. "I think we have much use for these two troublemakers than doing that do them." The older man says, holding up a piece of the explosive excitedly. "Even in this state, I can tell this was well crafted. It appears to be made to be non-lethal: just constructed to create a bit of unrest and chaos…." He explains to his son before looking down at the white-haired puca. "Is that correct ?" He asks Kaylan.

Nervously, Kaylan responds. "Yes…. that is correct."

"Like I thought… you're quite talented for one so young. I think we can offer you something better than a life weary tormenting travelers. Come with us, and we can help your talent flourish - you can work for us in the shop. It can be a way to repay us for damaging our things in the wagon." The older man says, looking down at the damaged cargo, offering them a deal. Kaylan hastily pulls Declan's arm, getting his face away from their view and closer to him so they can converse unheard. "We have to take this offer." Kaylan says in a whisper. "Why… why should we go along with some humans?" Declan asks coldly, in a hushed voice.

"I saw what they were carrying - he must be a sorcerer of some sort. He can teach me. I have always wanted to learn magic for as long as I can remember. Can you please do this for me?" Kaylan asks, pleading. "Fine … fine, I'm only doing this because you're my friend, but I'm not going to like this." Declan replies, pushing Kaylan back playfully.

"You have a deal." Declan declares, walking up to the older man. "The name's Declan, and that is Kaylan over there; it's a pleasure to come along with you guys." He says, showing a cheerful demeanor on his pale face. "A good choice, my boys, I'm Ronan Lynch, and you already know my son's name. I'm sure we will work well together." Ronan says, glad at their response.

"Good… Conor comes back into the wagon. We're heading back on this track to our new home with some new help." Ronan calls out to his son, sitting at the front of the wagon.

Conor climbs up to sit next to his father, quickly looking behind him for a moment with disdain in his eyes that these two pucas are coming with them. Declan lays back in the wagon restfully while Kaylan just sits there smiling at his new life. He looks closely at these two men's faces, having never really paid attention to how the people they pulled their hijinks on looked. Ronan is a robust and broad man with unruly, long, greying brown hair, a beard, and knowledgeable-looking light blue eyes. Conor is a scrawny, tall young man with short, neat, golden brown hair and determined hazel eyes focused on the path ahead. He watches them, taking in the appearances of the ones he will be living and working with for a long time, adding them to his very dear memories.

Settling into the house situated at the edge of Callunaton with everything packed and placed, Kaylan and Declan make themselves at home in the attic they were given to sleep in while Ronan and Conor each get their own room.

Declan is outside climbing around the outside of the house. He looks on at all the other dwellings hanging onto the roof. He hasn't been in the village, always looking in from the outside. There are so many humans walking around here, going about their day. Declan ponders, snickering under his breath.

"Enjoying the sights, puca?" Conor calls up from the ground. Declan gracefully jumps down next to him. "Never thought I'd get to come inside the village." The puca says, his eyes still wandering, observing everything around him. "When will we have the thing you humans call dinner… I'm starving." Declan says, grinning at the thought. "Not yet; we do that after the sun sets," Conor responds, amused by his eagerness.

"Fantastic, it isn't long from now?" Declan says, leaping up against the wall and hurriedly climbs back onto the roof. "Tell me when it is ready." He says, looking down at him before dashing off.

Conor just laughs at the puca's antics, going back inside the house.

Kaylan reads in the kitchen out of one of the spell books Ronan gave him, which he asked to study. He skims through the pages, reading up on all the different classes of magic: elemental, mind, enhancement, transformation, and reality, with each having different branches and types associated with each, and how you can combine these classes to create a variety of exciting spells.

"Here you go, my boy." Ronan comes over, placing a smooth black rock on the kitchen table. "Are you ready to see what magic class you are best attuned for?" Ronan says, gesturing at the rock. "Sure, what must I do?" Kaylan replies enthusiastically. "You have to hold your hand on a bit above the aptus stone; if it levitates, it in mind; if it changes shape, it's transformation; if it becomes heavier, it is an enchantment; if it is elemental, it will glow, and finally, if it a reality, it will distort the air around it." He explains what he has to do and everything he needs to know about it. Kaylan does just that easily because he is a magical creature.

It slowly moves around, slightly tilting, and starts to move off the table till it hangs mid-air…. levitating. Seeing this, Kaylan takes his hands away, letting it drop. He looks up to Ronan, smiling widely, happy at his result. "It's mind - wonderful! A class that's well attuned to intellectuals… Perfect, I will start your lessons tomorrow. Know this: you can also learn other magic classes along with this one. It becomes harder to learn and use classes of magic further from your own class though; it goes down from elemental, enchantment, mind, transformation…. with reality being the hardest to master, no matter which one you are attuned to… only those blessed with that class can use it properly." Ronan says proudly. "I will have to plan your lesson schedule now; maybe you could help me craft magical items for my shop tomorrow as well." He says, walking out of the kitchen, leaving the puca alone so he can continue reading the book.

"Ouch!" Kaylan yells out as a pebble hits him on the back of the head. He rubs the sore spot where the projectile struck him, turning around to see Conor standing at the kitchen entrance.

"Really struck gold by targeting us during how to move here, puca. Got yourself a house for you and your friend to stay in and my father to teach you magic." Conor says smugly, going up to the puca. "Do you have any problem with me being here? If so, we can talk about it?" Kaylan asks, confused by his attitude. "No… no problem at all, I was just messing with you…. I've never had the talent for magic; Father would enjoy having you around. I just came here to ask you something; you can see this as paying back our generosity towards you and your friend." Conor asks, having already forgiven what both of them did.

"With what do you need my help with?" Kaylan asks politely.

"I wouldn't be able to do it, and father won't do it for me. I ask you if you can make… me a magical creation…. to bring back the dead ?" Conor requests Kaylan earnestly. "Do you mean necromancy?… because whoever you bring back won't be like they used to be… they will come back a mindless pawn… without their soul." Kaylan says, trying to figure out what he is speaking of. "No, I want you to create something in order to bring someone back from the dead, along with their consciousness." Conor says, adamant about this goal. "I can try researching, try to look for some way to accomplish this. It does seem dangerous though and will take time as it has never been done before… we must take our time, not just rush into this." Kaylan replies, unsure of what he will have to do but really wanting to help the son of the man who gave him these opportunities.

"I'm sure you can do it. My father will teach you well, and you do seem quite intelligent, so please take your time." He says as he walks out of the room. "Oh, one more thing - don't tell my father of our plan. When we finish it, he will thank us later, so keep it a secret." Conor says, peaking back quickly before finally leaving.

In the attic, sitting on top of a blanket with a pillow behind him - they didn't have beds for them - Kaylan thinks that this will have to do for now until they can get them. It's small but cozy, with a desk with a chair to write at and a wardrobe with better clothes for them to wear. Kaylan looks up to the ceiling, pondering what to do. Ronan certainly wouldn't have any books to do with raising the dead.

He doesn't seem like the sort to dabble in such things. "Now that that was a nice meal." Declan says from the other side of the room. He lays down on his blanket and pillow with his hands folded behind his head. "I had my doubts, but this might, in fact, be great for us." The dark-haired puca says, content with their new situation.

"I thought you didn't like humans?" Kaylan hesitantly asks. "…. I still do….. it's just, I can see when I end up in an amazing new situation, even if it involves humans…. don't you think this is fantastic here." Declan answers him quickly, trying to explain to him.

"Yes, it will be fine indeed. Just hope it will stay this way now that we're here." Kaylan says unconvinced he hasn't warmed up to this family. Slowly, he looks back towards Declan, who has now fallen fast asleep. How strange, Kaylan ponders. He had never fallen asleep that fast before; he really had gotten comfortable in this place. "Goodnight then." Kaylan says quietly, trying to go to sleep himself.

Carrying a heavy satchel across his back, Conor walks up the candle-lit stairs to his room. Taking in every aspect of the old house he had returned to after so many years, having avoided it along with his father for so long.

Coming up around a corner, he walks right into his father, accidentally knocking into him and making him drop what he was carrying. "Sorry, father. I didn't see you coming." Conor says, hastily crouching down to pick it up. Getting back up with it in hand, he investigates what it is….. it's a miniature portrait wrapped up in cloth. He uncovers it, revealing a painting of his family when all of them were still together.

His attention is drawn to his mother standing next to his father, her curly black hair tied into a high bun, framing her fair, freckled face with her caring hazel-colored eyes, wearing an orange and green dress decorated with a flowery pattern with a leather vest over it. Standing in front of her is his brother, with his mother's hand placed on his wild mop of brown hair, wearing an oversized green tunic matching his eye color.

"Can you please give that back to me ?" Ronan asks him kindly. Snapping Conor out of his thoughts, he hastily holds the portrait out to his father. "Sorry again, just got a bit lost there….. seeing them." He explains in a melancholy tone and with a false smile, trying to hide his sadness at the memories of his lost family. "I know how you feel, my son. I have been feeling the same ever since we got here… all the memories of this place are flooding back." Ronan thoughtfully says, gently taking the portrait back from his hands.

"Still, it's great to be back, father….. to finally face and accept what happened…. yet I never thought it would be this difficult, though." Conor says, downhearted. He looks past Ronan with a lost expression. "It will get easier; we'll get through this together like always." Ronan comforts him, reassuring his son he will be there for him as they adjust back into their old home, which was abandoned when his wife and his youngest son died years ago.

"This will be a new beginning for us, my son. Along with the puca boys…. things will change for the better, I promise." Ronan goes on, placing his hand on Conor's right arm. "But for now, it's getting late, and it has been a long journey to get here. I think we better get some sleep; we have a busy day ahead." Ronan warmly says as he walks past him. "Of course, I just have a small something I have to do first." Conor replies, leaning slightly against the wall as he holds his hand. "Just try not to keep yourself up too long on one of your little projects." His father says as he goes to the door of his room.

"Sure thing, I'll try my best…. not to get carried away again, father…. hopefully." Conor assures him, walking up to his own room. Ronan just gives a knowing nod as he enters his bedroom, closing the door behind him.

He is confident that his son will get carried away again and stay up late like always.

The next morning, their first full day with the Lynches lies ahead. Kaylan is busy in the house's arcane workshop, surrounded by crates and cabinets of materials he needs to craft magical objects that will be sold at the small family shop. He sits in front of a large table with different kinds of crystal tools scattered across it. Kaylan carefully uses a crystal knife to carve swirling patterns into a block of greenish-black wood.

Ronan carefully instructed him on everything he had to make out of these mana-charged shield blocks before he left to open the shop. Arcane devices one can activate with a press to create a magical shield around a wide area, protecting the user. It is a great thing to protect those who can't use magic or a weapon to defend themselves. He'll just have to make about seven of these, and then later, Ronan will start their lessons.

Crash!…… Clang!……

Kaylan flinches in surprise, looking over to the noise source coming from the right side door. "Can you please be more careful to look where you are walking? Those are fragile!" He hears Ronan yell out from the second floor. "I was being careful, just got…. distracted; it's not like I'm going to do….." Declan shouts back, stopping mid-sentence.

Thud!….. Crack!…..

Kaylan sees a crate fall behind the open door, and Declan stumbles after it. "Seriously, you did it again and… right after you told me you're going to be careful." A tired-looking Conor says in disbelief as he walks up next to him, holding onto a bag. Declan swiftly picks the crate up. "Sure… I wasn't, still look, it isn't all broken." He says innocently, picking up the lid of the crate to look inside with Conor looking over him - Declan's eyes widen in horror. He hastily slams the lid shut, turning around to Conor sheepishly. "Like I said before…. most of it is fine." Declan says with a nervous smile. "Right, I'll just have to carry that to the shop as well." Conor pries the damaged crate from a reluctant Declan. Turning around with it, he notices Kaylan watching them from his chair, curious about what they are doing.

"Hey, Kaylan. Can't you help me out with moving these to the store in one piece? Declan has been getting too distracted while carrying the products." Conor asks him, gesturing back at Declan. "No…. sorry, this will take some time, then Master Ronan will start teaching me how to properly use magic. So I don't have much time to help…" Kaylan replies timidly, a tad worried he will be mad that he can't help out.

Conor thinks for a while, looking back at Declan, who is trying to take the crate from underneath his right arm. "That's fine; that just means I have to keep a closer eye on Captain Scatterbrained over here." He gestures back at Declan, who has given up on getting the crate back from him and is now playfully throwing a stone wolf artifact in the air and catching it. Kaylan nods in agreement, relieved he wasn't upset. "Declan, why won't you go up and get the bag of metal ores?….. you can take that to the shop." Conor says, confident he won't break that. "Right, I'll do that." Declan answers immediately as he tosses the artifact, walking up the stairs. Conor swiftly catches the artifact in mid-air. "Is he always like that?" Conor asks Kaylan as he places the artifact back on a shelf. "Practically every day…. I guess." Kaylan meekly replies, as he returns back to the contraption he was busy with.

"Great…. that will surely make working with him every day quite tough…. but at least it's going to be interesting." Conor says, trying to be optimistic about it. "That's a nice way of seeing it." Kaylan remarks, painting into the swirls he carved with a special kind of luminescent emerald paint.
Declan comes back down the stairs, holding the bag across his back. "I got it. Are we going now?" Declan asks impatiently to finish what Ronan sent them there to retrieve so he can have more time to explore the village. "Right, sure thing." Conor answers him before looking back over at Kaylan. "See you later." He says, waving as he leaves out the door with Declan.

Kaylan slices a square hole right through the center of the contraption. He embeds a peridot on top of the piece he sliced out, then carves the same spiral pattern on it, which he also paints. Kaylan places the sliced piece back in its hole and then sticks the cube firmly onto an obsidian base with a sap-like substance. He does this again and again, creating the rest of the mana-charged shield blocks, carefully making each one. Unaware of Conor and Declan, as they come back now and then to pick up more crates and bags of things for the shop. Hours go by till he eventually completes the consignment. Kaylan then rests a bit in the living room, letting the time pass by reading a book of psychic spells until Ronan comes home.

"Reading up today's lessons, aren't you? Well done. Your thirst for knowledge will make my job leagues easier." Ronan chirps as he walks into the room. "Thanks….. I wanted to get an early start, Master Ronan." Kaylan says politely. Ronan goes over to the puca, sitting next to him. "Let's start then with the most basic psychic spell." Ronan says, placing a silver apple on the table. "You must levitate this - high up." He explains. "You have to focus on it… imagine your mana reaching out of you, as invisible tendrils…. reaching towards the apple and lifting it up." Ronan instructs him.

Kaylan does as he was told, his eyes focused on the silver apple. It starts to wobble around a bit as he struggles to move it…. then slowly rises a little off the surface. It shakes as it floats upwards, stopping its ascent for a moment….. then falls back onto the table….. Kaylan stares intently at the silver apple, reviewing in his mind... on why he failed. "Decent first attempt, my boy. Now you just have to try that repeatedly until you master it - then we'll move on." Ronan encourages him to stick to it.

Kaylan directs his focus back onto the apple, trying to levitate it again. Failing and beginning again, working to master this spell through the entire evening until it becomes night. Eventually, he manages to levitate the silver apple for a few moments... till it drops down once more. "Well done, that will be all for today. We shall continue the lesson tomorrow." Ronan says, content with the puca's progress. "I think I'll get the hang of it then." Kaylan says seriously. "I'm sure you will." Ronan exclaims, patting Kaylan's back. He stands up, looking in the direction of the kitchen.

"Oh…. I almost forgot it was late and hadn't prepared dinner yet. I'll leave you be then, my boy." Ronan says, leaving Kaylan to read the book he was busy with much earlier. The day is almost over, his first full day with them. Kaylan ponders, excited for what awaits him. What he will experience and learn in the days to come.

CHAPTER 21
Nothing lasts forever

Five years have passed, and Kaylan was taught well in the arcane arts. He even got Declan to learn with him while Kaylan was instructed to send messages to others through his mind, levitating objects, and so forth. Declan was taught cryomancy as he was discovered to be more attuned to the elemental class. Declan was hesitant to learn magic seriously but ended up enjoying it the more he learned. On the side, Kaylan was secretly studying how to create the thing that would bring the dead back along with their minds. Kaylan found books on the matter every chance he got, building up his knowledge. He and Declan also have gotten very close to Conor over the years.

They became increasingly like brothers, going out every day just to do something fun, like exploring the forest and discovering interesting things, racing with horses, fishing, or going out for a drink. With Ronan seeing both Kaylan and Declan more like sons, they really had become a family of sorts.

In the midst of autumn and in the early morning hours, underneath a lone Sycamore tree outside the village, Kaylan puts the finishing touches on his the magical creation he has been working for for so long. It looks like a cylinder - a bit narrower at the top, made of some kind of hard purple material with strands of banshee hair weaved all around it like a net, and a pair of golden clawed hands with strange engravings on them, holding onto the top from a golden and obsidian base. Kaylan places a translucent gem containing a black liquid shaped like a skull in a slot on top of it.

Kaylan sits in his satchel, swinging it over his shoulder, walking down the hill. "Winters coming early this year!" He hears Declan shouting down the hill. Running about shooting ice and snow across the ground with his arcane weapon, he received a silver scepter with a larimar stone on top.... only a few days back. Really testing what it can do after learning to use his magic with it properly. Now, his spells are much more potent because of it. Declan has done things similar to this before.... after he learned a new spell. Going out to play around with it. He used to do it in the village a couple of years ago but was convinced not to anymore by Ronan after many angry complaints from the villagers about having parts of their homes frozen over.

Kaylan walks past him, almost getting hit by a blast of snow. "Kaylan, feeling like joining me in a friendly little snowball fight?" Declan asks, pointing his scepter at him as a challenge. Kaylan replies timidly to his question, explaining why he can't join. "I don't have time to join you… sorry. It is my turn to work behind the counter at the shop today."

"Your loss, pal." Declan says smugly.

"I can play along at midday when Conor takes over. If you're still going to be here." Kaylan says, feeling a bit guilty for saying no. "I will be here all day; I'm having too much fun with this," Declan replies. Kaylan walks away, going to the village, hearing Declan excitedly yelling out to him. "See you later when I beat you in an avalanche of snowballs!"

Kaylan walks into the Arcane supplies stop, the shop owned by Ronan. It's a quaint little store with a nicely carved wooden sign again above the door, showing potions, gems, metal ores, and sage along with a mortar and pestle with the name of the place next to all of it on this sign. Kaylan goes behind the counter; he puts his satchel down before sitting down on the chair. Placing one of his arms up on the counter, he lays his head against his hands as he waits for the shop to open.

"Good morning, my boy." Ronan says as he comes from the back door. Kaylan sits up straight. "Didn't think you'd be in the shop today so early." The young puca says, taken by him being there now. "Just had to get one thing from the storage." Ronan says warmly. "How does your arcane weapon feel ?" He asks Kaylan as he goes up to him. He looks down on his right arm at the copper brace with a purple lepidolite embedded in the middle. Kaylan replies. "Amazing, practiced with it last night." Using it to telekinetically let a ruby float over to his hand, grabbing it from the air, all of this done so effortlessly.

"Nice…. and I know you will do much greater in the future than mastering such a basic spell." Ronan responds.

Kaylan hands the ruby to him. Ronan then places it back on the shelf. "And I will put the hard work in to reach my full potential. For myself and for you, Master Lynch." Kaylan says adamantly. "Good then, I'll return to the house to craft more stock and let you return to your work… before any customers arrive. See you later, my boy." Ronan says as he waves goodbye, walking out of the shop.

Kaylan went on with the day, working behind the counter. I sold things, helped customers choose what kind of gem and metal ore combination would be perfect for their arcane weapon, and quickly restocks the fennel and rue. Going on with this work until it was the middle of the day.

Conor walks in as Kaylan is done dealing with a customer. "Conor, can I talk to you briefly in the storage?" The puca asks when he comes to stand at the front of the counter. "It's to do with the project of ours." Kaylan adds as he picks up his satchel. "Sure, I'm coming." Conor says, nodding. Kaylan leads him through a door at the back. Now, away from prying eyes, they can talk. "It's ready, I call it the Saola contraption." Kaylan says, taking it out from the satchel. "Nice, how does it work ?" Conor asks, looking happier than he'd ever been. "That's the thing, I'll have to activate it. You know, since you're not… capable in magic." Kaylan says, placing it back in the satchel. "Right." Conor replies knowingly.

"So what is the plan? Where do I have to use it ?" Kaylan says, wanting to get this over with. "Go to the village's cemetery at midnight. I will be there, ready and waiting." Conor responds, excited at what's to come.

"I'll see you there." Kaylan timidly says as Conor walks out, and he goes out later to see Declan. Wondering about his way, in every way this might go wrong, hoping he can pull it off.

Hiding behind a pillar of ice, a flurry of snow blasts past him, with the sun setting behind him. Kaylan waits for an opportunity. As the blast of snow stops, he rolls out. Using his telekinesis to pick up and form a giant snowball, he hurls it towards Declan. Kaylan's opponent jumps out of the way of this projectile, sending back a hail of snow. "Let's see you dodge that." Declan shouts out confidently.

At the last moment, Kaylan ducks down, letting it shoot over him. Catching it with his telekinetic magic, he sends it back, blasting Declan far away to the other side of the field. Kaylan stands up, smiling. As he sees, Declan bursts out of the giant pile of snow, defeated in this match. "And tha….. that is what I…. call… a win." Kaylan says shakily, shivering from the cold. "That was a fun match." Declan shouts out, getting out of the snow. Shaking it all off from him. Declan runs up to Kaylan, grinning widely; Declan gives a quick bow. "Well done, but I will be the winner next time." He says cheekily.

"I'm certain you will, considering your progress in cryomancy, I am sure in time…" Kaylan says, about to ramble on. "Sure… sure, but now we got to get back home." Declan says, interrupting him. Kaylan looks at him, his head cocked to the side in disbelief that he interrupted him. "I haven't had a thing to eat in a while… dinner has to be ready now." Declan says, running past him. "You coming along, Kaylan?" Declan asks, looking back. "Yeah, I'll be right behind." Kaylan says as he shakes off the disbelief.

Back in their house, with all of them seated around the dining table with a bowl of potato leek soup. Conversing with each other when they are not busy eating. "Anything interesting happened today?" Ronan asks Kaylan, not getting a response. He asks again, snapping Kaylan out of his thoughts. "Oh….. right…. after I tended the shop, Declan and I had a little fun with a competitive snowball fight." Kaylan says, stirring his spoon around in the soup. "Who won then?" Ronan chips in, interested to know. "Kaylan…. kind of did." Declan says, looking a bit embarrassed by this.

"Well done, Kaylan. I'm sure Declan put up a good fight." Ronan says, getting Declan's attention. "Of course, I did, like always." He answers to Ronan quickly, holding up his fist with enthusiasm.

"Wouldn't have expected any less." Ronan says warmly. Looking on at both of the pucas with pride. "Father, sorry to interrupt your conversation, but I can say something." Conor asks very politely. "Sure." Ronan replies. Conor closes his eyes before speaking up. "Father…. I have something special planned for you that I think you'll enjoy, a gift."

"What is this gift? I'm quite intrigued?" Ronan asks, awfully curious.

"That's a surprise, father. You'll see what it is soon; you're definitely going to love it." Conor responds, chuckling, as he sits back in his chair. As Kaylan watches him closely, quite certain what he is talking about.

Deep in the cold night with the moon high up in the cloudy sky, Kaylan stands next to his bed in the attic, illuminated by a little amount of light coming in from a round window in the middle of the attic, streaming through. The satchel with the Saola contraption in it strapped around him. He quietly walks out of the room, not to wake up Declan. Checking behind him as he closes the door gently. As it shuts, Declan's eyes open up, turning his head towards it as he gets up.

Kaylan runs out of the house and moves about the village's mist-covered streets. Holding his satchel close to him as he walks out of Callunaton. Going up a hill towards a small fenced-up area. Kaylan pushes open the large steel gate, heading inside. He moves slowly around the cemetery, looking around carefully for Conor. He walks carefully around the tombstones, the ground covered in fog like the village. "Up here!" Conor shouts out, standing next to two coffins further along the cemetery. Kaylan sprints over to him, taking out the Saola contraption and looking around nervously as he does it. "Is this the people… you're trying to bring back?" Kaylan asks timidly, staring down at the closed coffins next to a set of tombstones with holes dug out in front of each. On one is inscribed Maeve Lynch, and on the other Rory Lynch. "Yes… there's my mother and… little brother, lost to me ages ago." Conor says sorrowfully.

"But now they are going to come back, and our family will be whole again, thanks to you. I'm certain they will like you, especially mother... she has a curious mind just like you." He goes on, his face lighting up with hope and joy as he says it.

Kaylan smiles at this, happy at his approval… but something is in the back of his mind, nagging at him to stop this. "Are you certain you want to go through with this? It might not work…" he begs Conor. "I am, this will work… I have faith in your abilities." Conor replies, not showing any doubt.

"Right." Kaylan says as he carefully places the Saola contraption between the two coffins; he walks back a fair bit with Conor standing behind him. Kaylan gives a heavy sigh, taking a flask of white glowing liquid. He opens it up, dipping one of his fingers in it. He takes it out and paints a line across his brace.

Kaylan holds the hand with the brace forward towards the Saola contraption as his hand begins to glow white. A glowing symbol starts to form in the air in front of him. It is of a crescent moon and a spiral next to it in the sun, with a star on the top, left, right, and bottom of it. A glowing beam shoots out from it to the Saola contraption. Slowly, it lights up - one by one, the golden clawed hands let go of the cylinder. Falling down to the ground. A translucent sphere starts forming from it, expanding outward.... until it covers both coffins within what appears to be a glowing bubble, pulsing with tiny electrical sparks across it. Conor looks at it in wonder as Kaylan speaks out a single word. "Fillenobis, rise!"

A blue light swirls around in the sphere, getting increasingly intense. As the coffins levitates a small bit off the ground, the ground inside the sphere begins to shrivel and die. Kaylan looks on in horror as a mighty wind, along with the fog around them, is trying to pull them in. Something is going wrong; this isn't supposed to happen. Kaylan thinks as he tries resisting the pull, along with Conor. "What is going on? Is this supposed to happen?" Conor yells out to him, confused. "This… this isn't how the spell is meant to go…. it's trying to to get more mana… it doesn't have enough to achieve its goal…. and we are the nearest things with the most mana… it will suck us in and drain the life out of us both, along with it." Kaylan yells back, still keeping himself firmly in place.

Conor looks on at the Saola contraption with the swirling light crashing around it violently. "What are we supposed…" He tries to yell out Kaylan, his words lost in the wind. He can't hear himself - this magic is silencing things around him.

Kaylan looks around frantically at the Saola contraption, trying for a way to stop it until he's eyes fall…. Declan…. Declan… Declan is coming towards them on the other side of the sphere.

Desperately, Kaylan shouts out to warn him, flailing his hands in the air desperately…. but no sound comes out of his mouth…. What is he going to do there? If he tries to run to him, he will just be sucked in…. Declan will… Declan will… go into that thing, not knowing…! Thoughts race across his head as he stands there. Feeling utterly hopeless, he tries to use his telekinesis to throw Declan, but it's not working…. is the Saola contraption suppressing his magic.

Feeling Conor's hand on his shoulder, he looks over to him. He can see his mouth move but can't hear anything. Conor gives a weak smile as he runs past him… towards the sphere, holding a rock…. smashing the Saola contraption to pieces as his body ages rapidly before his eyes……

Kaylan yells out, holding out his hands. As a massive flash of light bursts out from the explosion…. covering his whole field of vision…. blown back into a tombstone….. knocking him out.

Kaylan weakly opens his eyes to look on at a depressing scene of destruction, as tiny flecks of light rain from the dark night sky above. He gets up, holding onto his head, which is burning intensely with pain…. Kaylan notices that his bracer is gone from his arm…. what happened to it? Did that explosion have something to do with it? He thinks…. slowly remembering what just happened.

He rushes over to the spot where the Saola contraption was, hoping that what he saw... what happened didn't just happen... only for his heart to be crushed…. by the sight before him.

Lying alone, with the coffins wholly gone. In a heap lays the corpse of….. his dear friend and brother… Conor, with a ball made of purple lepidolite, is lying beside him. He falls down next to him, clutching onto his old, frail body, drained from all life…. pressing it against his own…. he looks down at his lifeless visage, crying in silence…. tears stream down his face. Declan stands a distance away from them, and he calls out in disbelief. "What… what have you done?" As Declan falls down to his knees, looking on in pained sorrow.

Kaylan just looks back, unable to say even one word to him.

CHAPTER 22
The beginning of our training regiment

"After.... that I ran away scared away with Declan.... scared of what Master Ronan would think... Declan then left me shortly after, blaming me for it all and why shouldn't he.... because of my inadequacy, Conor died." Kaylan confesses pitifully, slumped over in the chair.

Sitting on the low table, Kamaria looks him in the eyes. Seeing all the pain and sadness within him, she hadn't really noticed before. "I understand how you feel, but it wasn't your fault; you couldn't have foreseen that happening." She says, trying to comfort him. "But I could have saved him; he shouldn't have had to sacrifice himself... for me." Kaylan retorts bitterly as he looks away from her. Kamaria places her hand on his face. "It was his choice to save you and Declan.... it was such a tragic thing that happened.

Would he have wanted you to carry this guilt with you for the rest of your life?" She tries to reason with him, only getting a similar result. "I just can't…. bring myself to do that…. if I was only better, I could have prevented it in the first place." Kaylan says, pushing away her hand.

Kamaria watches him sadly. "I think you should return to Callunaton and talk to Ronan." She says, having come to a conclusion. A look of terror forms on Kaylan's face as he bolts up from his seat, walking away from her. "I don't have it in me to face him, no I can't… he would be crushed… if I told him what I did." Kaylan clutches anxiously onto the mind orb. "He seems to really care about you…. Kaylan, you must talk to him for Ronan's and your own sake." Kamaria pleads.

Kaylan just stands there, staring away ahead of him. "Right…. I'll go, it's just..." He responds hesitantly. Kamaria goes over to him, putting her arm around his back. "It's going to be fine…. you're not going there alone." She says, getting a slight smile from him. "We just have to inform Master Glynn at the training grounds where we are heading." Kaylan nods in acceptance of what he will have to face.

Situated in a lush valley, seven cube-shaped buildings constructed of limestone and granite stand large against the black Alder trees, forming their surroundings beside a gentle river. Outside one of these buildings, Oran is talking to Fritz and Blaire. "Each of you will undergo rigorous training exercises for about ten days. Every one of you will work on improving yourselves." Oran says, pointing at Blaire first. "You'll be working on reducing your mana consumption with spells and having the capability to have multiple portals open at once." He says as he summons a strange large dog with a whip-like tail, glowing white eyes, and a glossy black, red, and blue pelt with a white underbelly. "This is Failinis; he'll help you with your training." Oran introduces the hound. "How is some weird-looking mutt going to help me improve ?" Blaire asks, confused at this. "I am no ordinary dog, you whelp!" Failinis yells at her with purple lightning arcing around its back, offended by her comment.

Blaire takes a few steps back in fright at the hound speaking. "Sorry….
uh…. Failinis, I won't say anything rude again." She says, a bit
embarrassed.

The hound walks up to her, staring at her. "Come now…. follow me; you
have much to improve in a short time." Blaire follows him away into one of
the buildings. Now that they are gone, Oran goes over to Fritz. "You will
have to improve your skills with melee and long-range weapons combat, as
well as increase your physical strength by your efforts and enhancement
spells." Oran tells him, summoning a muscular humanoid dark grey wolf
wearing only a torn olive green cloak and worn-out red trousers. "This is
Darragh; he's a man-wolf. He's a fine warrior and will help your training
excellently." Oran says, introducing him. "I can tell." Fritz says, smirking
while looking Darragh over, from the top to the bottom. "Come with me,
human. Your training begins now, and I won't go easy on you." Darragh
says, leading a cheerful Fritz away into another one of the blocky buildings.

In the furthest building, Atgeir and Leifur enter a vast room, the floor made
of a smooth purple-black stone with large pillars and rocks sticking out in
certain spots. It has an incredibly high ceiling and is entirely foggy white in
color, matching the walls; every now and then, red and pink lights streak
across it with trails of glowing dust. At the far end of this room is a high-up
lookout structure made of dark wood and blueish metal against the wall
with stairs leading to it.

"Today will be your first day of intense arcane training, and I won't go easy
on you just because you're my little brother!" Leifur says as he walks to the
middle of the room while conjuring his strange-looking lute. "It will be a
very tough and grueling challenge, but when you come out of this, you'll be
immensely stronger than before; you will improve old skills and learn new
ones!" Leifur goes on trying to hype him up with a bit of flair. Atgeir just
looks on at this, unimpressed. "Are we going to start now, or are you just
going to keep running your mouth." Atgeir says scornfully. Leifur is a little
taken aback by this. Still, it is expected that he is still mad at him for what
he did. "I see……your training will be… to fight against me while using
your electromancy, in tandem with speed and including reflex-enhancing
spells…. That's not it - you'll also have to try and fight back with electric

spells…. you'll do this for hours and hours, practically most of the day until it doesn't put much strain on your body anymore …. this will make you faster and strengthen your very mana, making your spells stronger…. Then we'll move on to something bigger for the rest of the time we have left." Leifur lays forth his entire plan for Atgeir exercises.

"And how long will this take then?" Atgeir asks skeptically. "About six to eight days, then I will teach the bigger thing I was talking about - an ultima spell that I'm sure is well suited for you…. during the rest of the days we have left, as I mentioned." Leifur says, confident in his method. A strenuous and challenging method he learned about in the realm he visited to speed up his arcane training.

Atgeir gets into a fighting stance, holding both the spells he was asked for at the ready. "Let's do it then. I'll definitely going to end this thing much earlier." Atgeir says arrogantly. "That's bold of you to say I'd missed your over-confidence. This will be fun sparring with you again, like old times." Leifur chirps. He gets into a fighting stance as well. He plays a note on his lute, sending a powerful sound wave. Atgeir dashes off to the side, dodging at incredible speed. He lets the sound wave smash a pillar behind him to bits. Atgeir sprints swiftly towards Leifur, ready with an electrified punch.

Leaning up against one of the structures, Oran Glynn watches Kaylan and Kamaria approach him. "Salutations, I assume the problem is dealt with." Oran says, glad to see them. "Not really, Master Glynn." Kamaria answers with a friendly bow in greeting. "What do you mean by that?" Oran asks.

"Kaylan has to talk to someone from his past… to finally move on." Kamaria says, turning her gaze back to her puca friend, standing slouched over, glancing up at her nervously. "I'm going along with him…. for support." She tells Oran her plan. "No, I'll go go with him." Oran responds, pointing to Kamaria. "We don't have much time to train each one of you. You will be trained by one of my summons." He says, unwavering in his instruction.

"I understand, Master Glynn….. just wish I could have gone with him."
Kamaria says feebly with a lowered head, wanting to be there for her friend
in that decisive moment. "It is a shame. I don't have much of a choice here,
do I." Oran says as he summons a fairy out of a puff of smoke. It is a small
thing; its skin is a light glittering violet, and it has large yellowish orange
eyes framed by long dark purple hair, tight back in a bun. It wears a dress
made of bluebell petals with a pair of shimmering yellow dragonfly-like
wings on its back. "I am known as Aoife; don't be fooled by my petite
stature. My magic makes me more than a match for anyone." The fairy
says, giving a curtsey while she flies in front of Kamaria's gaze. "I am
called forth to help improve your reflexes and accuracy with fast-moving
targets as long as you learn magnificent spells to use in close combat."
Aoife says, explaining her purpose here.

"Such a pleasure to meet you, Aoife. I will enjoy learning from you."
Kamaria says, giving a curtsey back to show her respect for the fairy who
will train her. "Now, come on with me, my dear." Aoife says, flying off in a
blur of light. Kamaria quickly looks back to her friend. Kaylan nods sadly
back to her, showing he is okay with it. Kamaria runs off, leaving him to go
with Oran, while she enters one of the cube-like buildings to train for the
fight ahead.

As they start their training, far away in the cave far above the mountain, the
Blood chimera sits crossed-legged, surrounded by its terror beasts, the ones
who attacked Astera Bay with him. A dark form bolts into the cave, in a
blur. It stops before the chimera, revealing itself as the very creature that
clung onto Blaire…. Dark.

The chimera gets up, its eyes locked onto the tiny monster's form, with all
the beasts around him turning their heads to it. The chimera goes down to
its knees, giving a bow with its wings spread down. Dark begins to grow
bigger and bigger, with its features contorting and changing as it does. Until
it reaches its full height, in the form of an unnaturally thin man - the skin is
a leathery grey with a fading purple hue. Its eyes are still cavernous voids
with a small white light within each. The top of its head was covered in oily

reddish-black hair with jagged spikes poking out from underneath it. The man wears a robe made entirely out of black and yellow smoke. "You have done well; now you just need to finish the job." Dark says, its voice a cold, droning tone.

"I will master…. I just have to wait…. So I can finish my target off…. At it's strongest." The chimera replies with a broken voice. Grinning savagely at the mere thought of his future battle. Dark strokes the chimera's chin with its bony claws. "You always enjoyed the thrill of the fight…. your greatest weakness, unable to finish someone off as instructed. You just have to get your way." Dark says menacingly, scratching at the chimera's face, scarring him. The chimera pulls away from…. him before reeling back in pain. "I will do as you wish, master….. only with my method." The chimera replies back, grinning widely as he holds onto his injured face, pitch black blood dripping from between his fingers. "You better, my child… this is the very…. sole purpose of you even existing." Dark says, disappointed at his beastly-looking offspring. "I will come back later to see the results." He waves farewell with a clawed hand and….. vanishes out of the cave in a burst of shadows.

"I won't be defeated…. he will be the one…. who will be defeated… when you finally return to me." The chimera says, keeping its terrifying grin.

CHAPTER 23
The then and now

Five years ago, on that horrible night in the Thiar realm.

Kaylan dashes frantically across the moonlit fields along with Declan running close behind him, his eyes filled with tears and breathing heavily. The orb he found next to Conor's body, now speedily levitating right next to his face, following him very closely. Kaylan keeps going on, further and further away from his old home, which feels lost to him forever. Until he can no longer go on….. suddenly, he collapses on the hard ground, utterly exhausted. Declan quickly stops beside him, trying to catch his breath, slouched over and just as tired as Kaylan. Declan scornfully looks down at his friend, with whom he has spent most of his life. Pulling himself together, Declan starts to walk away.

"Where are you going…. don't go, please... brother!" Kaylan desperately shouts out, reaching towards him. The dark-haired puca stops in his tracks, staring back at him. "No… I'm not!" Declan snaps at him, turning around to look directly at the distraught Kaylan. "Not after what you did…. because of you, Conor is dead and…. Ronan will never forgive us; I was there, too…. and I couldn't do anything." He tells Kaylan in a pained tone, keeping back his tears. "I can't go with you… can't even go back home… I will just have to go somewhere away from here… it doesn't matter." Declan says coldly as he goes back to walking away from him. "Please, I don't know what to do. I can't get through this without you….." Kaylan says weakly with his head lowered to the ground, scared of ending up alone, especially after what he had witnessed and done.

Declan sadly shakes his head at the miserable sight of his now former friend. "Goodbye Kaylan and sorry…. I just can't stay with you….. because I can't forgive you for what you did; how could you have been so careless... to do such a sick... sick thing." He says, running off into the darkness of the night, the light of the moon now completely blocked by clouds, leaving Kaylan all alone on the grassy hill with the dim glow of the mind orb shining against him as he wraps his arms around himself in a hug, trying difficultly to give some comfort to himself. "It wasn't….. I didn't….. no, it couldn't….." Kaylan mutters quietly, closing his eyes tightly.

"No, it can't be….. but it is….. it truly is…. it is all my fault. He is gone because of me." Kaylan says weakly, feeling truly defeated and in utter despair.... surrounded by a cold darkness…. empty and numb….

Feeling hollow……

Thiar realm, back in the present….

"Never been to Callunaton myself, heard it is a quaint little village. I suspect from the story you told me that it won't be all cheery bells and whistles for your return to the place." Oran says, noticing how Kaylan anxiously trembles as he walks ahead. "It will be…. painfully difficult… but I have to do it, to move on….. to improve." Kaylan replies sadly but with a glimmer of hope in his tone. Kaylan walks further ahead of Oran, trembling even more as he sees his old village as they move over the top of a hill. It all is so familiar - the smell of the flowers, the sounds of the specific birds of this area, and the sight of the lone sycamore tree on the hill in the distance, where Kaylan often sat in its shade reading or crafting something. As they enter the village, he takes in different sensations with his heightened senses. The smells of bread being made in a bakery, the sound of talking and people going about their daily routines, and the sight of the well in the center of this village, where he, Conor, and Declan regularly sat together. They just have a bit to eat together after work or talk to each other about what happened to them that day and what fun thing to do next.

Finally making their way to Kaylan's old house, the puca looks on at it with utter dread. His rabbit-like ears are drooping down, a look of pure terror on his rounded face. He takes in all aspects of the house - the grey brick it is made of, the faded blue tiled roof, and the door's shape. All of this brings back happy memories, only to be crushed again by the memory of his last night here. Kaylan tries to instinctively run away, only to be grabbed by his collar by Oran. "Hold it, Kaylan, you are not going anywhere." His master says, pulling Kaylan to the front door of the house. "Sorry…. I couldn't stop myself there…" Kaylan says weakly, feeling overwhelmed.

"No need to fret - just means I have to keep an eye on you so you won't run away from confronting this." Oran says jokingly, trying to put his former apprentice at ease.

"Thanks, Master Glynn… I'm glad you came." Kaylan says timidly as he knocks hesitantly on the door, waiting anxiously for Ronan to open. Scared of what will happen next, if it will officially sever his and Ronan's bond forever.

"Maybe he is working late at the shop; we should come later..." Kaylan makes an excuse, trying to walk away again. Oran grabs onto his arm as the bronze doorknob starts to turn. Kaylan freezes, scared stiff, as he hears the door open. "Kaylan… it's really you!" He hears Ronan yell out to him. Kaylan looks back hesitantly, seeing Ronan. He appears old and wrinkled but smiling widely at the sight of the puca. "Hi…." Kaylan says weakly, waving his hand slightly. Unsure what to say, Ronan embraces him with a bear hug. "You're back, my boy…. you're finally back home, after all these years…. You're here." Ronan says tearfully, his heart filled with joy.

Kaylan gently pushes him away. "I am glad to see you again too, but I have…. something I have to do first…" He says difficultly, looking at Ronan, who is waiting to hear what he will say. He glances at his master, fearful of what he has to do. Oran gives him a look of encouragement, reassuring him to do what has to be done. Giving a heavy sigh, Kaylan moves his gaze back to Ronan. "I have to tell you something…. something I should have told you long ago." Kaylan lowers his head in sorrow, knowing what he will have to say.

All the rock structures and pillars lay strewn and shattered inside the building where Leifur and Atgeir went to train. Dashing across the room, Atgeir dodges his brother's volley of destructive sound wave attacks. Atgeir leaps out of the way of a sound blast, jumping against the wall behind him and into the cover of a half-broken pillar. He catches his breath a bit. Crouched down, he holds onto his chest. His whole body aches and tires from continuously using enhancement spells and his electromancy to send electricity through his body, enhancing his reflexes and speed even more. His body isn't used to such strain.

Atgeir runs out from his cover towards Leifur, and another sound blast gets shot at him. Atgeir slides down and under the range of the attack and kicks upwards in a burst of crimson lighting at Leifur's back. Leifur spins around, blocking it with his hand, holding onto his leg. Atgeir points a finger at Leifur, shooting a small lightning bolt at his face. Leifur lets go of him, and Atgeir hastily stumbles away, running off to a safe distance.

"I can see you're beginning to tire out, but your training ain't done for today." Leifur says, getting a sharp retort from Atgeir. "I'm not done yet…. I'm not someone who just gives up so quickly, or did you forget it after you ran away from us."

In his fury, Atgeir shoots eight lightning strips at Leifur, who just leaps across it as the attack tears the ground below him. Leifur plays a chord on his lute, shooting a sound blast in mid-air at Atgeir. Holding his gauntlets up, Atgeir blocks the attack. The force of it pushes him back against the wall. He stands there, disorientated by the attack; Atgeir leans back on the wall. He hastily shakes off this sensation. Atgeir runs at Leifur, dodging a sound blast. Atgeir punches at him, his gauntlets enveloped in scarlet electricity. Leifur sidesteps it, punching Atgeir back in the stomach. Stepping back, Atgeir places his hands on both of Leifur's shoulders, sending electricity through him. Leifur yelps out in pain. He grabs onto Atgeir's shoulder with his free hand, grinning cheekily. Leifur headbutts him, and Atgeir instantly lets go of his shoulders. Leifur kicks him off of him as he punches forward at Atgeir.

His attack is blocked by one of Atgeir's gauntlets. Using an electrified roundhouse kick, he counters but misses Leifur. Playing a couple of chords on his lute, he sends a large blast of sound back, sending Atgeir shooting back into a rock structure, smashing it to bits as he crashes through it. Atgeir skids to a stop on the ground.

Atgeir crawls back up in a struggle, still keeping his spells up despite the severe pain and heavy fatigue. "You are not going to wear me down that easily!" Atgeir yells. Leifur smiles at his brother's determination. "You were always one to never give up. It will make things easier." He replies with a little chuckle. Atgeir runs back at Leifur, continuing their fight. They go on the whole day - back and forth, with Leifur attacking Atgeir, with him dodging these attacks and fighting back when there is an opening. This goes on and on till it becomes dark outside.

Atgeir collapses on the floor, completely exhausted. "That's the first training day - it was too easy." Atgeir tries to hide his exhaustion. "Really, it looked more like you were struggling through training." Leifur says, standing next to him. "Hilarious… you must have mistook my actions for your difficulties keeping up or your exhaustion." Atgeir retorts, sitting up straight and pretending to laugh. Leifur shrugs off this comment, as his brother will never openly admit his faults. "We'll just have to see how fast you finish this part of your training… How long will you think you'll take?" Leifur says teasingly at his brother's bravado.

"I'll say it will take about five days tops, then I'll just have to use a couple of days to master that ultima spell you want to teach me… then I'll have time to rest before my battle with the Blood Chimera." Atgeir responds nonchalantly, his demeanor entirely free of any doubt.

"Sure you will, Geir." Leifur exclaims with a hint of sarcasm. Getting an angry glare from Atgeir, who immediately picked up on his tone. "Now, where are we going to sleep?" Atgeir asks, too tired to argue, pointing at Leifur. "You don't expect me to go sleep on the floor." Atgeir complains. "That actually sounds like a swell idea…. but Oran told me there are beds in that enclosed outlook over there, so I think I'd rather rest there." Leifur answers him, adding a little joke along with it. Atgeir gets back up shakily, trying to steady himself so his brother doesn't see how worn out today's training made him. They head to the stairs, walking past the devastated floor with ruined pillars and rock structures. The structure magically begins to slowly regenerate to what it was. Piece by piece, along with broken parts of the walls, shifting back into position like puzzle pieces.

They walk into the lookout with two beds and a metal-enforced wooden crate. Small lights float around this area, with more drifting about the rest of this large room.

Leifur opens up the chest, seeing bags filled with loaves of bread, oatcakes, pickled fish, cured meat, and containers filled with water. "Looks like we don't have to worry about not having any food here." Leifur says, looking back at Atgeir, sitting on one of the beds, not even paying attention to his brother's words. Instead, he is inspecting the bed closely. Feeling the mattress and the covers - it will have to suffice for the next ten days, Atgeir thinks. "Do you want to maybe... continue where we left off with our talk?" Leifur asks him, unsure why Atgeir hasn't tried to talk about it till they meet up in Astera Bay. He sits on the other bed, holding onto an oatcake, waiting for an answer.

"So, are you ready to apologize for what you did and return home with me? I'm listening." Atgeir responds smugly. Laying on his side, holding a hand

close to his ear to show he is waiting intently….. "No, why would I do that
?!" Leifur yells out, annoyed. "I'm not going to do no such thing; all I
wanted to do was try and reach some kind of understanding between us."
Leifur goes on, gesturing frantically as he speaks. "There is nothing you
could possibly say or do that will make me change how I feel about this. I'm
not just going to back up on this, just like I suspect you won't either." Atgeir
retorts, turning away from him. "You just have to make things more
difficult, do you. Just can't admit it when you're wrong." Leifur says with
his arms crossed…. no answer or witty remark; Atgeir is giving him the
silent treatment. This will just have to be resolved slowly throughout his
training. His brother can be stubborn and prideful, but maybe, at the very
least, across their days training together, he might change his stance just by
spending time together and seeing how much better things there are for
Leifur.

Sitting at the dining table of his old home, with Oran sitting right next to
him and his old master Ronan seated on the opposite side, Kaylan looks at
this old, shriveled-looking man before him, listening in sorrowful silence.
"So I ran… Ran far away from you… Because it was all my fault that….
He died…. Why Conor died." Kaylan says tearfully, with his head lowered,
fists clenched and placed on the table surface. Bracing himself for Ronan's
anger and betrayal-filled words, only to hear nothing from him. "Why aren't
you saying anything…." Kaylan says, looking right into Ronan's sad eyes.
"I should pay for what I did; if I only had been better, made the Saola
contraption right, he would have still been here….. I could have just
stopped and not even made it in the first place…." Kaylan clenches his
hands, slamming his fist on the table in pained frustration. "I deserve only
the worst from you…. For my inadequacy and cowardice." Kaylan
concludes with his head slumped onto the table, sobbing.

Feeling a gentle hand on his head, Kaylan looks up. "Get up… my boy."
Ronan says in a melancholy state. "The years after my son's passing were
absolutely miserable, caused by that heart-wrenching experience… When I
saw him there…. Dead…. Unable to recognize him when I first laid eyes

on…. His body…." The old man says, holding a hand to his chest. "But I don't blame you for what happened; Conor chose to save you… No matter what caused that catastrophic incident…" Ronan now looks at Kaylan, who is now sitting up. Trying to comprehend why Ronan is being so amiable to him, as he is directly looking into his eyes. "I will forgive you like my son would have…. as he was always a kind and forgiving young man….. if you care for him as much as I do, you can't keep blaming yourself." Ronan says in a caring manner, holding onto Kaylan's hand.

Looking down at this kind gesture, Kaylan smiles slightly. Tearing up again, remembering Conor and what he was like. Ronan tries to get a word to comfort him but gets…. stopped before he can. "That doesn't make it less sad to me…." Kaylan says miserably. "…but I'll move on for Conor's sake…. as he would have wanted, I don't want to squander his sacrifice…. by wallowing in pity my entire life." Kaylan says timidly with a somewhat hopeful tone now.

Ronan gives him an emphatic look, aware of how both of them have suffered because of this. Just want his and Kaylan's mental scars to heal on their own time, not to keep clinging to the traumas of the past. Ronan had experienced these feelings more than twice, having long to think about them over and over again and learning to go on while still keeping the ones he loved in his memories.

CHAPTER 24
Pushing through

Fritz sits against the wall of the room, eating a loaf of bread with slices of meat in it, which he made from what he found in their chest. Darragh is still sleeping on the lookout. They have stayed up much longer working on Fritz's training until midnight. Still, Fritz got up quite early, having felt hungry from not eating the night before. He had just gone to sleep after hours of strenuous training.

Fritz takes a swig from a bottle of whiskey. He found it at the bottom of the chest. A great find, Fritz joyfully thinks. On the wall, a glowing pink portal appears next to him; from it, Blaire peaks out. Looking about the room, she notices Fritz. "There you are !" Blaire yells out in glee. She leaps out of the portal, landing in front of him. "Come to see me, B. Can't blame you.… I'm an absolute hoot to be around." Fritz says, making a silly face. "Yeah, sure. Whatever you say…." She says, rolling her eyes at his cheekiness. "So, how's things going here? Must be better than training under Failinis ?" Blaire asks, frowning with her arms crossed. "Better than what you are going through, I can imagine, then again. You ain't someone that likes any kind of hard work," Fritz answers, adding a light-hearted remark.

"Hey, that's rude, Fritz….. true, but still, you could have said it nicer….Then again, never mind… ugh !" Blaire shouts frantically at him, irritated. "Maybe, but I feel telling something upfront is way better." Fritz says in a relaxed manner as he hands over the bottle of whiskey to her. Blaire takes a drink from it. "Thanks, I'm already feeling tired of this training." She says, handing it back to Fritz. "It won't last that long, and when all this is over, I'm definitely just going to settle somewhere and do absolutely nothing. It will be a life of rest and relaxation every single day from then on. I won't become a soldier again…. like back then.... never again." Blaire smiles widely as she tells him, her hands placed to her sides.

"That's a nice enough plan and all, but not my idea of a great time…." Fritz remarks, interrupted by furious barking from some distance behind them. "Looks like your pooch is calling you back for practice." Fritz says, pointing back. Blaire's expression turns into a look of apprehension. "Right…. see you later." Blaire says with a strained smile; she opens up one of her portals, reluctantly jumping into it.

Now that Blaire has left, Fritz Picks up the empty whiskey bottle and heads back to the lookout. He snickers a bit under his breath as he ascends the stairs at the thought of Blaire having to actually do hard work. As Fritz enters, he sees Darragh still asleep on the floor. The wolf seems to like sleeping on the ground more than on the bed. Then again, he does seem the beastly sort to prefer that. He looks so peaceful resting there that Fritz kind of feels like trying it himself.

Fritz takes a loaf of bread from the chest before sitting on the floor beside his bed. There is still some time to kill, waiting for Darragh to wake up. Better eat another bite and rest a bit more for the day ahead.

Kamaria stands atop one of the pillars in her training room, pondering how Kaylan is doing. Wondering if he's doing well and if he has reconciled with his past, would that old man truly forgive him for what he did? Kamaria doesn't know if she could forgive if someone did the same to her - then again, it isn't her doing - the forgiving.

"Kamaria.... Kamaria!" Aoife yells out to her, snapping her out of her thoughts. Kamaria looks down at the fairy fluttering around below, waiting impatiently on her. Kamaria hastily climbs down to her; she looks on at Aoife, feeling a bit embarrassed. "I was just contemplating something, master Aoife." Kamaria explains why she was up there, holding her hands behind her back. "You are feeling concerned for your friend, aren't you?" Aoife asks, flying closer to her face. "That's correct; I can't hide from a fairy how I feel." Kamaria responds immediately, well aware of the natural ability of their kind to sense one's emotions, and she can't hide it from Aoife. "That's so adorable how you care for your friend... just don't let these feelings distract you." The fairy tells her sternly. Kamaria manifests two curved swords of light, holding them at the hilts, showing Aoife that she is ready for their training to commence. "It won't, Master Aoife!" Kamaria exclaims.

"Well said, now we can begin today's sparring practices." Aoife says, cloaking her body in an armor of shimmering pink light, as she takes out a small knife made of brass with a pink coral gem on its hilt. Aoife flies at Kamaria at an incredible speed with a "whirrrr" of her wings, her knife ready! The light shield Kamaria manifested just in time blocks the attack at the last second. Kamaria dissipates the shield, slashing forward with a blade of light. Aoife flies out of the way and slashes Kamaria's face. Taking the opportunity, Kamaria hits her away with the broad side of her light blade. The fairy tumbles through the air, stopping some distance away from Kamaria. Aoife flies back speedily, ready with her blade.

They continue fighting, trading countless blows. Kamaria keeps a defensive stance, forming shields to block the fairy's strikes, and when there is an opening, she strikes back. As it goes on, Kamaria's reflexes and perception are slowly improving, becoming more capable of making split-second decisions in combat.

Atgeir dashes around the room, evading Leifur's sound blasts. The attacks left behind small shattered craters on the floor. Leifur pursues him, jumping from pillar to pillar. Playing on his lute to create a new sound wave attack again and again. Atgeir retaliates repeatedly in a burst of scarlet electricity at his brother. He uses a crimson lighting-charged kick to the base of the pillar Leifur is standing on, obliterating it. Atgeir's opponent leaps off as the pillar crumbles.

Atgeir runs up to his brother, slashing upwards with his electric-covered clawed gauntlets. Leifur dodges this, moving around his attack swiftly. He tries to jab at Atgeir, only for it to miss him. Atgeir moves out of the way, punching Leifur in the jaw. Stepping back a bit dazed, Leifur holds his face, grinning. "Now you're getting better, Geir. Not a lot, but you're getting there; I felt it a little through the invisible mana armor around me." Leifur says enthusiastically. This constant enhancement spell makes you tougher against attacks and is used throughout an entire fight. It can become stronger slowly over time, making you capable of tanking more damage before breaking. Leifur's is quite strong - and Atgeir's will become just as strong in time.

Atgeir smirked smugly at his brother's words of praise, a part of him still caring about what Leifur thought. "Of course I did, and that's just the start." Atgeir says cockily, still in a fighting stance. Leifur sees his brother's over-confidence radiating in its glowing opportunities.

That isn't necessarily bad; we just have to see if he can keep that attitude up with this training regiment, Leifur thinks as he plays a chord, sending out a sound wave slicing vertically across the room. Breaking the ground through it, Atgeir dashes away from its path.

His body still feels a strained pain all across his body, and Atgeir keeps pushing through it. He knows that if he keeps moving through, it will no longer affect him in a few full days of this arduous training. Atgeir rushes to his opponent, keeping himself close to the floor. He creates small balls of lighting on the tips of his clawed gauntlets, throwing all of them ahead of him. Leifur dodges swiftly between these orbs, a couple only making tiny tears in his clothes as each whizzes past. Atgeir comes up from behind these projectiles, punching at him. Leifur blocks this with his hand before striking back. Atgeir ducks beneath it, striking back. So they go on, trading blows, blocking and weaving around each other's attacks. Leifur ends this, kicking forward. He pushes Atgeir back, getting enough time to grab his lute. He plays a chord, shooting out a sound blast. Atgeir stumbles out of the way, just in time.

Atgeir runs off, away from Leifur. He just has to avoid some of those relentless barrages of sound waves. Atgeir's body still feels that constant stinging pain during it all. Yet he persists, now and then, yelling out things at Leifur. "Is that the best you can do!" or "This is getting way too easy, Leifur !" Words said to psych himself up more than anything else so he can continue longer. No matter how he feels during it, he must go on. He is starting to enjoy training with his brother and spending time with him after so long... Atgeir could get used to this feeling.

Things are really moving along; he won't just stop now; he's someone who will never give up on something Atgeir really wants, and now he wants the power to slay the Blood chimera.

CHAPTER 25
Moving on with you in my heart

Around six years ago, in the Thiar realm.... inside the vast forest near the village of Callunaton.

Kaylan rests near a lake, lying comfortably on the grass bank near the water, feeling a gentle breeze caressing his face and the sun's warmth. He looks over to see Conor sitting beside Declan, who's holding onto a fishing pole. Watching intently at the water, impatient to catch a fish. "When is the stupid fish going to bite? We've been here for hours…. this is getting super boring, Conor." Declan says, frustrated by nothing happening. "They will, eventually." Conor replies calmly, his eyes closed. Declan looks over to him, frowning at Conor. "Eventually… that can take forever!" Declan irritatingly says. In a relaxed fashion, Conor sighs. "You might or might not catch anything today, but I think the wait is the best part…. just taking in your surroundings. Catching anything is just a bonus. That was at least what I was taught." Conor says calmly, playing around with a reed between his fingers.

Declan watches him, puzzled by his sentiment. "I'd rather just have the fish than some boring experience where I just sit about at a lake with nothing happening for hours." His gaze gets pulled back by the water, searching for any fish near his hook. He notices a dark shape moving further away in the water. Declan grins mischievously; it's a fish. "Conor, come and look. I'll show how someone catches a fish and how a puca does it. That's way faster than using some pole with some flimsy string." Declan announces confidently, throwing away the fishing pole. He shapeshifts into his dark wolf form, leaping into the cold water. Splashing about as he tries to bite at the water, at his prey.

Kaylan rushes to Conor to watch Declan's wild attempts to go after the fish. Conor has come out of his relaxed state, keeping his eyes locked onto Declan while smiling at the absurdity of him going after the fish so doggedly. The fish breaches out of the water as Declan bites down at the water, where his prey is— getting slapped back in the face by its tail fin. The fish falls back into the water, swimming off to escape its tenacious predator.

Declan sits down in the water, panting frantically. Feeling a fish swim near him, he bites into the water beside him. Ending up in biting down on a stick draped in wet grass and weeds, instead of a fish.

Declan scornfully glares at them, from the water. He growls at his laughing friends, embarrassed by his current situation and soaking wet. Angrily dropping the stick back into the water, the puca starts to skulk his way out of….

Clasp!… a pair of green scaly, webbed hands grab onto the dark puca's waist… digging its sharp claws into his sides….

Declan yelps out in pain…. as he is forcefully pulled backward deeper into the murky lake… Desperately he plants himself firmly in place, clawing into the lake's muddy bank, so he won't get dragged in anymore…. the puca fearfully looks back to the sight of two vicious bulging red eyes on a scaled spike-covered head, snarling hungrily at him with rows of needle-like black teeth. Frantically he bites at the monster. Yet all these attacks do, is barely make it even flinch… failing, the scaled beast just starts to pull harder onto him, dragging the puca deeper in the water.

"Declan, I have you!" Conor swiftly grabs onto his neck, pulling back with all his might against the monster's immense strength. "Kaylan…. Kaylan…. Kaylan!" Conor yells back to a frozen-in-place Kaylan, frightened and unsure of how to act. All the white-haired puca does is stare in stunned silence. "Kaylan…. do something…. use your magic…. anything!" Conor yells out to him again, struggling to keep his footing in the loose mud as the monster bites at him. Conor quickly grabs the stick floating next to him, shoving it in the creature's maw.

"Uh… I… uh… right." Kaylan hesitantly says, shaking it off his "Right, I'm coming!" He yells, running off towards them, fuelled by pure adrenaline. Sliding down next to them, he places the palm of his hand on the monster's spiked forehead.

Kaylan suddenly…. sends a powerful psychic wave straight forward, the monster is launched away from them in a thunderous boom! Sending it, plummeting into the inside the waters on the other end of the lake.

Staring ahead…. entirely out of breath. The three, sit there in the water, soaking wet but relieved. Carefully watching as the monster's head peaks back up from the lake, snarling at them as it submerges back into the murk… furious at what Kaylan did, yet now scarred and scared of them. Conor gives a sigh of relief petting Declan in his wolf state, getting a frustrated glare in return from the dark-haired puca. Declan stumbles out of the lake, shape-shifting in a puff of smoke into his normal form. Conor comes up from the water as well, followed by a shaken Kaylan.

Conor suddenly burst into a fit of laughter, catching both of his friends off guard. "What are you doing…. have you gone mad, I almost got killed, and you're laughing!" Declan

"Sorry…. sorry… I mean it." Conor says, trying to stop himself from laughing anymore at how he looked in the lake. "It's just I couldn't help myself. It is bizarre, you looked so ridiculous, splashing about in the lake after that trout then this monster just comes launching out of nowhere…. it felt terrifying but exciting at the same time…. what I mean, I guess it was just the suddenness of it all." Conor tries to explain himself, having finally stopped his laughter.

Declan gets up slowly, violently shaking all the water off him. Splashing it all over, Kaylan and Conor, standing nearby, are holding their hand in front of them, trying to block themselves from getting wet. "Weird…. still, I kind of get it…... I just couldn't help myself from feeling mad at it, just like you strangely couldn't from laughing at it." Declan says while trying to dry out his tail. "I guess so, I didn't think you'd say something so understanding and deductive... It looks like Father and Kaylan's ways of thinking are rubbing off on you…. isn't it?" Conor says sheepishly. "No, I'm not… I'm not turning into some brainy bookworm!" Declan yells out, embarrassed that he would think such a thing. "Why do you think that's a bad thing…. to be like that." Conor asks, confused as to why he's so mad at what he said.

"What…. It's because…. Uh…. I don't know." Declan says, not finding any word to say about it. Feeling ashamed, he turns away from both Conor and Kaylan.

"Don't you think we should go back home? This fishing trip went seriously wrong, we got attacked. We cannot salvage that... there is no point in trying to recover this." Declan suggests strongly, grabbing onto both of them. He tries to drag them along with him away from there. "That can't be right; we still have the fishing pole. You can just pick it up and resume with our somewhere else with fewer monsters…." Kaylan brings up, pointing to the fishing pole lying near the lake. Declan swiftly turns around, blasting the fishing pole into pieces with a fast ice projectile. They look at Declan with shock as he turns back to them with a grin. "Oops… Didn't mean to do that…. reflexes, I guess." With a cheery attitude, Declan holds onto the back of his head.

"Wasn't that our only fishing pole?" Kaylan says as he stares back at the shattered pole. Conor places his hand on Kaylan's back. "It's not much of a loss; we can get another. Either by making a new one or buying one with a coin saved up from working at the shop… We can even get more than one, so all can fish together," Conor tells him. Kaylan looks back at him happily, thinking that they will return here in the future; it looks quite relaxing to sit there contemplating things among the trees. Declan could learn to like it, and then they will have another thing they can enjoy together.

"Are you two coming or what!" Declan yells out to them, gesturing to hurry up. "We're coming, you hyperactive puca!" Conor shouts back, grabbing Kaylan's hand. "Come on, Kaylan. We better get going before Declan drags us with him by our collars back home." Conor says jokingly. Kaylan nods with a smile, running right next to him, after Declan, who is sprinting away, far ahead of them.

Back in the present, Kaylan stands at the grave of his deceased friend and brother. Holding tightly onto the mind orb in his hands, Ronan stands beside him. It has been four days since he came back to his old home. They talked to each other daily about all their happy memories with Conor. The good and even the bad memories, each one of them. It is worth remembering, as each is a precious piece of him they will carry with them forever. Conor's grave rests close to that of his mother and brother; at least he got to be with them in the end. Kaylan has finally brought them here to see Conor's final resting place.

"I found this orb of purple lepidolite near…. Conor, that day…. It has followed behind me ever since. The only thing I could move around with my mind anymore after that dreadful night." Kaylan says solemnly, letting go of the orb. He points where he wants it to go, and the sphere flies off. Going around in circles and different patterns, go along where Kaylan points. He returns it to his hands, and then Kaylan turns to Ronan.

"I don't know why it got there…. Still, sometimes I feel like, with this…. He's still with me in a sense; I can't explain it." Kaylan says, carefully considering his words as he speaks it. Holding tighter onto the orb held between his arms. "I think I know what you mean…. Even if I don't think I understand it myself." Ronan replies, gazing down at the tombstone. Made devotedly by his own hands from the stone in the surrounding area, as he did for his wife and Rory, something he had to do for them. From a deep need to honor them and show how much they meant to him, a way to remember them. This isn't the same, but could Kaylan's magic subconsciously have made it, in the moment, to preserve Conor, in a sense. Yet, Ronan thinks of this as… just himself being too hopeful. Then again, there is no reason it isn't so?

"When I found him that night, I could immediately tell it was him, even though he was aged appearance…. He seemed content in his actions, in peace…. His soul now in a better place, the Great Beyond." Ronan says, crouching down to place a flower on Conor's grave.

"That's comforting to think about, still doesn't make me miss him any less…." Kaylan timidly says, closing his eyes for a moment. "Sorry…. Master Ronan, can you please…. leave me alone to be with him for a moment?" Kaylan asks with his head hanging to the ground. "Of course, my boy…. take your time." Ronan responds, giving him a hug before leaving Kaylan without saying another word.

Now, in silence, alone. At that very exact spot, he lost Conor. Kaylan looks down at the tombstone. Holding the mind orb in front of him. "I'm back, Conor….. I don't know if you can hear me…. from beyond there, in the ether…." Kaylan speaks up, breaking the silence of the cemetery. "I'm going to become the strongest psychic this realm ever saw, learning everything there is to know about magic…. I'm not going to waste your sacrifice." Kaylan says, tearing up as he speaks. "I will become someone you would be proud to call your brother." He finishes, holding the mind orb back to his chest. Turning around to walk away, as he had said what he wanted to say to him…. suddenly, the Mind orb emanates a warm glow between his arms, the blue glow catching his attention and a strange sensation pulling him back. Kaylan looks at the sphere, bewildered. As a wave of lights penetrates into his very being, absorbing into him…. telling…. telling him…. to show what he is capable of.

Hesitantly, Kaylan starts to levitate the mind orb up above his head. Taking a deep breath, his hands glow the same color as the sphere. He sends the orb blasting ahead. Flying off above the ground with a thunderous boom. Leaves are being blown away by the force, and trees swaying back. It whizzes around him at blinding speeds, creating a trail of light that vanishes over time. Kaylan watches this, directing the sphere on where to go next. The entire time, he is certain that his brother is with him. That Kaylan just wasn't open enough to see it before. Now, he will live for both of them, seeing and experiencing what they always wanted to do.

CHAPTER 26
Persevering

Atgeir rolls out of the way of a sound blast, throwing balls of crimson lighting. Leifur ducks underneath them, still running opposite to him in the room. It doesn't feel as painful as when he started this training, but he can still feel the strain in his body. Today is the fifth day of his training; he can't take any longer to finish this part, or he will end up looking like a fool for predicting that he will take only till today to complete it. Atgeir runs after Leifur, keeping pace with his brother's incredible speed. Atgeir overtakes him, blocking his path. He kicks at Leifur's legs in a burst of scarlet electricity. Knocking his opponent off balance, Leifur stumbles ahead.

Regaining his footing, only to see Atgeir rushing in to swipe at him with his clawed gauntlet. Leifur steps back in the nick of time, avoiding the attack.

Atgeir has gotten much stronger these last few days, yet he still isn't ready to face the Blood chimera.

Atgeir kicks upwards in a crimson arc of lightning. Leifur grabs onto his leg with one hand, stopping it immediately. Leifur flinches in pain at the impact of catching his kick. Using his other hand, Leifur punches him, but Atgeir counters, shooting a bolt of lightning from both of his hands at his face. Freeing himself from Leifur's grasp. Atgeir steps a fair bit back, enveloping his gauntlets in electricity.

"That's about all for today's training." Leifur says, holding up a finger. "What! I was just about to defeat you and end this part of the training !" Atgeir shouts out in utter disbelief, walking closer to him. Leifur just sighs at this, holding his hand face in his hand. "The day is over, and it's dark out now. I won't just let you train yourself to into exhaustion…" Leifur says, pointing at him, raising an eyebrow. "You need your sleep for the next day's training." He expresses his concerns, showing he does not back down on this. Atgeir stares scornfully at Leifur for a while as he walks past him. "You're just afraid I was going to beat you just there." Atgeir says, thinking he got him. "One word, no! I'm not going to let you manipulate me. I know how you work, Geir." Leifur says smugly, ruffling Atgeir's hair as he walks near him. Atgeir glares coldly at his brother, lowering his head. Atgeir's expression changes as a sly grin shows on his face. "I guess you're right, Leifur. I'll just have to finish it tomorrow." Atgeir says while straightening out his hair.

Atgeir runs up the steps into the lookout, followed by Leifur. "You got over that quickly but didn't you have your sights set on ending part one today?…. exactly." Leifur asks, seeing Atgeir lying on the bed, eating a loaf of bread. "I was just one day off. Did I really say I would finish it in five….. I meant six." Atgeir responds nonchalantly as he rests his head back on a pillow, crossing his legs. "Right…" Leifur says, feeling slightly unconvinced of what he's saying. "I was just wondering, how did father take my disappearance?" Leifur asks. "When you left, Father led multiple search parties across the realm to search for you, not even looking for you in any other realm as he thought you were too young to go that far away…. years passed, and he gave up on finding you. Thought you died, and so he went and destroyed all the realm gates, scared that all the sulfrens that came into our realm from….. the others were the cause of your death, and he didn't want it to happen again….. to any of us. Isolating us from the rest of the known realms," Atgeir answers, keeping his gaze away from his brother. "That sounds about right for father; he always has to be in control of everything, to a ridiculous degree…. taking everyone's chance to explore other realms, he handled it poorly." Leifur scoffs. "What else could he have done? That was the most reasonable decision." Atgeir argues with him. "He could have just fought back at the sulfrens while mourning my loss quietly. He shouldn't just drag everyone in the Severne realm into this. Taking away their freedom to come and go as they please." Leifur says as he sits down on the other bed, taking out his lute. He plays it, sending out a gentle mist of light that swirls around the room. As a soothing melody accompanies it. Atgeir slowly starts to fall asleep; he places his hands over his ears for a moment, letting go of it slowly, to look over to his side…. until eventually, Atgeir falls asleep, Leifur looking over at him. Smiling, Leifur puts his lute down. He quickly takes something from the chest to eat before going off to sleep.

As the hours go by, Atgeir begins to stir. Opening his eyes, he sees Leifur is sound asleep. Atgeir slowly gets up, removing two pieces of red crystal from his ears, which he quickly formed with his mana. It blocked out Leifur's sleeping spell before it took hold of him. Just had to fake falling for it, and now the plan is in motion. Quietly, Atgeir slips out of the outlook, running across the room and outside. He is going out to train himself, so there will be no chance he won't beat Leifur tomorrow.

Underneath the partially cloudy moonlit night with the sounds of crickets chirping, breaking up the silence of the night, Kaylan and Oran stand at the door in front of Ronan's house. The warm light shines inside the open door, with Ronan standing in the door frame. "I'm deeply sorry that I can't stay much longer…. I can't just take care of a few things, then I'll be back… I promise." Kaylan says meekly, his ears drooping back sadly. "It's fine, my boy, do what you must do first. I'm not going anywhere." Ronan sympathetically lets him know.

"Thanks, Master Ronan. I'll try to find Declan when I'm done aiding the slaying of the Blood chimera….. I'll Bring him back home." Kaylan says, holding his hand up to his chest. "While you are gone, I look forward to seeing… both of you again." Ronan says warmly, hugging Kaylan.

Ronan then goes over to Oran. "It was a pleasure to meet you, I have heard great things about you and your past endeavors…. your capture of the Oilliphéist at the great Aster Lake was astonishing." Ronan says, cheerfully shaking his hand. "That water serpent was a tough one for sure; it took some creative thinking to catch… now it's one of my best summons." Oran says proudly, grinning arrogantly as he recalls that mission. When he was still a young apprentice. "I wish we had more time to talk to you about other of your arcane discoveries. I do enjoy discussing every aspect of magic there is." Ronan says wistfully. Thinking of all the magical knowledge that someone of such renown as Oran knows.

"I could come around in the future when Kaylan returns. It would be interesting to see how much he has improved." Oran says confidently that Kaylan will become a great sorcerer.

"That will be amazing…. my friend. I won't keep you up much longer…. you have Kaylan to prepare for a battle." Ronan says. "Thanks for your hospitality, farewell." Oran says as he walks away with Kaylan. Waving goodbye as they go off along the path till they are out of sight of Ronan. Heading back to ready themselves for the great battle ahead.

As the sun rises, it announces a new day. In every structure along the river, everyone is training hard to improve their capabilities, even Blaire, who is trying her best. Inside the one closest to the river, Atgeir and Leifur stand as opposed to one another, posed and ready to fight. Leifur observes his brother closely. He looks much more tired than usual, yet still, he seems more confident and resolute than ever.

Atgeir runs straight at him, his body enveloped in a cloak of scarlet electricity. He bursts forward in a fury ball of lightning. Leifur holds up his arms, blocking Atgeir as he comes out of the flying sphere of electricity, punching him with an explosive force that knocks Leifur meters backward. Manifesting his lute, Leifur plays a chord. Shooting out a sound blast, Atgeir stands still. Enveloping his left arm with electricity, he waits till the blast reaches him. He shops horizontally across the air at it in an arc, creating a broad shield of electricity in front of him. Dispelling his attack as it collides with it. Atgeir dashes through the shield of electricity, clearing it out of the way and cloaking himself in it. Atgeir runs at Leifur, jabbing at him rabidly, his opponent dodging them until the final one lands on his right shoulder.

Leifur counters back by slamming his lute at Atgeir's side, the instrument covered in a protective mana barrier so it won't break. Knocking Atgeir away momentarily, Leifur quickly steps back to get some distance between them.

Atgeir lunges at Leifur, dodging past a sound blast attack. Going up to him, he jabs at him, with Leifur blocking it and striking back swiftly. Atgeir avoids it and punches back. So they go on striking at each other while trying to dodge and weave out the other attacks. Leifur dodges a left hook, giving him an opening to grab hold of his lute, playing a chord that sends a sound wave. Pushing Atgeir back a bit, Leifur takes this opportunity to run off. Atgeir dashes after him, in pursuit up the wall. Leifur keeps running to the wall, going right up it with Atgeir following behind him. They run across the walls, Atgeir shooting off a small lighting sphere at Leifur ahead of him. Only one of these projectiles hit him. Still, it's not stopping him from keeping up his speed. Atgeir hastily pushes off the wall in a burst of crimson lighting and launches himself straight ahead. Slamming straight into Leifur, they plummet down. Atgeir grips tightly onto Leifur's neck, punching him rapidly in the face with his electrified gauntlet.

Both of them crash to the ground in a loud, shuddering thud.

Atgeir stands crouched on top of Leifur. Still holding onto his throat, Leifur just grins back at his brother; he is ready. "You can let go of me, you did it… you won." Leifur says cheerfully. Atgeir lets go of him, jumping off from Leifur. He goes to sit down next to him, snickering under his breath. "I did it; I had no doubt about it… I told you so." Atgeir says, ecstatic at his victory.

"Well done…. then again." Leifur says as he gets up. "You did get some extra hours of training in last night." He mentions as he tries healing the wounds on his arms with a spell. Atgeir stares at him. "You knew I sneaked out to train?" Atgeir asks in disbelief. "Of course I knew, I stayed up a while longer to make sure. You didn't pull something off to prevent my sleeping spell from working; I saw you leave." Leifur says calmly, touching his badly bruised face. "Then again, I'm glad I decided not to stop you. It really paid off; it was the push you needed to win…. you're now ten times faster and stronger than you'd ever been." Leifur explains as he tries to heal his battered and bruised face. "You just allowed me to get past you, to do what I wanted." Atgeir questions him, confused as to why he let him train that night when he clearly said yesterday he shouldn't have. "I thought about it, and I'd rather not take on your training like father did with me…. controlling and restrictive, on what you can and can't do. I knew you wouldn't go out there and train yourself to an absolutely exhausted state."

Atgeir looks at his brother, stunned by what he said. Unsure of what to even say about it. "Still, I think you should rest the remainder of this day, then we can start your training with the ultima spell tomorrow…. does it sound like an acceptable plan to you ?" Leifur asks him understandingly. Atgeir gives a confident smirk. "I guess it's a fine plan….. Very well, I'll get some rest." Atgeir says, keeping his confident demeanor. "Great… you'll be well rested for tomorrow's training. I'm positive you're really going to like this spell I'm going to teach you; it will fit you quite well…. it's immensely powerful." Leifur says, enthusiastic to teach his little brother this fantastic spell.

"I always knew I'd beat you eventually, Leifur!" Atgeir confidently says, chuckling at the mere thought. Receiving a surprised but knowing look from his brother. "Good for you… too bad it will be your last victory against me, Geir." Leifur boisterously tells him, well aware of Atgeir's nature.

"Are you challenging me… because I'm certainly going to make you regret that in the future, just you wait." He cockily replies with a big grin. "We'll see about that." Leifur states, just as excited for this challenge to come, as Atgeir is… to see who will come out on top next when all this trouble against the Blood Chimera is over and done, to challenge themselves and reach new heights.

CHAPTER 27
All set for battle

In the Severne realm, the Hyvits palace…

Thyra sneaks quietly behind her mother down the hallways of the palace. Sia walks gracefully down the hall, trying to keep her composure. As she gets more worried about Atgeir every passing day, he is gone. Wondering if he is okay, concerned he might have gotten horribly injured, and he isn't going to come back. She stumbles forward clumsily. Snapping her out of these terrible thoughts…. As she regains her footing, she turns around. Looking for what tripped her up there.

It's a servsi; she must have walked into him while she was deep in thought. The little golem hurriedly bows down. "My apologies, your highness. For my clumsiness, I failed to get out of your path. Forgive me for what I have done." The servsi asks pleadingly. Sia looks pitifully at the servsi. "You can take your leave servsi; just be more alert next time, and look out where you are walking next time." Sia says sternly, getting a grateful smile from the golem. "I am grateful for your kindness, your highness. I shalt not let this happen again." The servsi appreciatively says, giving another polite bow. It scurries off swiftly. Calmly, Sia moves on, unaware of Thyra following her, wondering why she hasn't said anything to her father about Atgeir. Thyra follows her to the large living room, peaking from the door leading into it. She suspects that her father is sitting on the couch in front of the fireplace, resting. He is usually busy all day, working on something.

"It's so nice to see you finally taking a break." Sia says as she sits on a coach close to him. "It's bizarre. There's nothing for me to do now; it feels strange." Eilif says wistfully, as he is not used to taking time off. "You could take me for a peaceful walk in the gardens." Sia suggests, leaning over to hold onto his arm. Eilif has his hands to his chin, thinking it through. "Sounds like a grand idea, Si…. The cold, fresh air of the morning hours will be…. invigorating. It will be nice…. especially with you being there with me." Eilif says in a caring manner. Trying to keep her happy, after Atgeir was sent away to the abyss defense tower, she felt off after he left, acting even more melancholic than ever. So when he has a chance, he tries to help her feel better.

"That's so sweet of you to say, my dear." Sia chirps, giving him a kiss on the cheek.

Thyra watches all this from behind the open door, careful not to let them see her. She wondered how long her mother would keep this secret from her father. She is confident it won't be long until she can't hide it forever. It's hard for her mother to keep secrets, and this secret must be weighing heavily on her.

Right back in the Thiar realm, in the valley.

Their preparation time is over, and everyone converses in front of these large cube structures. It was the first time anyone saw each other in almost two weeks.

"You just got to meet my former master, Ronan. I'm sure he'll love to meet you; you can come with me…. after I find Declan." Kaylan says excitably, holding out his hand and gesturing expressively. "That sounds lovely; seeing the man who taught you so much about magic will be interesting. From what you said, he seemed quite knowledgeable." Kamaria contently answers. I'm glad to see how happy Kaylan is acting now. "It would be nice to show you how better my arcane combat is now, but I'm not sure you'll notice while you're fighting a terror beast, too." Kaylan says, feeling a tad disappointed he won't be able to show her how he significantly improved anytime soon. Out of the corner of his eye, he notices Atgeir approaching them; he walks through them with Leifur following behind him, pushing Kaylan out of his way.

Kamaria gasps at Atgeir's disregard for Kaylan's feelings, shoving him to the side. "I'm not going to repeat it; you're coming back home with me." Atgeir retorts at his brother. "Like you will get it right to drag me back to the Severne realm." Leifur responds fiercely, striding away from him in a rush. Atgeir just stops in his tracks, crossing his arms. He watches Leifur leaving to talk to Oran. "That idiotic, headstrong fool." Atgeir says coldly, under his breath.

Kamaria walks up to Atgeir from behind, still angry for rudely pushing Kaylan to the side. The puca stops her, grabbing quickly onto her shoulder with his hand. "I'll talk to him." Kaylan tells her in a whisper. "Sure, go ahead." Kamaria says quietly back with an understanding nod; he can handle it now.

"Hi, I have noticed you are having trouble with your brother, making you more brash than usual." Kaylan carefully says, getting a scornful glare from him. "Creature, you know nothing of what you talk of. Don't mess in matters that don't involve you." Atgeir callously says. Kaylan just shrugs this off. "I don't know what you and Leifur are dealing with. Still, I am certain that you have to look closer to your brother's point of view before you just judge him….. you have to, or you might lose him." Kaylan tells him, looking up at Atgeir directly in the eyes. "What did you say, creature.

You know you are talking to, don't you ?" Atgeir says scornfully. "I do know, and I was saying you should try to understand your brother, or you might lose him. Do you really want that? Because I wouldn't." Kaylan answers fearlessly, holding his head high. He walks away, having said what he wanted to. Leaving behind a stunned Atgeir at the puca's attitude towards him and a sudden realization to do with Leifur that's starting to set in.

Atgeir shakes the thought off; this isn't time for this. He tells himself victory is close at hand, and he can't let some creature's words distract him now. Focused on his task ahead, he walks past Fritz and Blaire and over to Oran, who is busy talking with Leifur. "Are we going to head out yet? I'd rather get this battle over with, don't you?" Atgeir stoically asks Oran. "Just wanted for everyone to talk to each other before we left; I suppose they had enough time for that." Oran answers him calmly. Closing his eyes, he sends out a telepathic message to everyone there. {It's time to fall in. We're heading out now !} Slowly, everyone falls in behind Oran, heading westward to the mountain.

Fritz and Blaire walk along at the back. "We're finally going to end this stupid monster invasion. That dog trained me to exhaustion daily; I'm glad to have that far behind me." Blaire rambles on, complaining loudly about what she went through. "Did your stamina get any better then ?" Fritz nonchalantly asks, walking beside her. "Yeah, it's better now, but it wasn't fun at all to get there." Blaire replies, a tad annoyed by it. "Yeah, that ain't saying much coming from you." He says, yawning at the end. "Really… you know you can stop being rude about me being lazy. I just finished some grueling training, and I think I deserve that… In the least." Blaire says, cocking head. She frowns at his smug expression. "Uh…. right, I guess the joke was getting old. I better make a new one." Fritz says, cheekily bumping up against her. Blaire pushes him away. "Of course, you will…. you rogue." She says, smiling, having gotten used to his antics.

The entire group, led by Oran, walks out of the dense forest, with Atgeir and Leifur following behind him. Having trekked all the way from the valley in the easterly direction of Astera Bay. They are met by the Blood chimera resting up against the foot of the mountain. Surrounded by the terror beasts, he invaded the city alongside them. Including two new ones they haven't seen before…. A mantis-like terror beast with jaggedly sharp raptorial forelegs that glow a purple hue and a gigantic greenish thornback ray levitates in the air, with red stripes, yellow glowing spots going across, and a mace-like tail. This beast is entirely covered in a thin veil of yellow electricity.

The chimera rises from its resting spot, spreading its massive scarlet wings. It starts laughing as it walks closer, its eyes focused on Atgeir. "Follow me…. elf….. we fight, and the created beasts will…. deal with the rest of you." The chimera demands Atgeir in its broken tone, pointing at him with its claw. "Fine, I accept your terms." He agrees stoically to the monster. Atgeir quickly glances behind him at his brother before following the Blood Chimera right up the mountain. All the terror beasts look at the remaining people standing at once.

CHAPTER 28
Clashes around the western mountain

Oran steps forward, using his staff. He creates a sign with light summoning a giant emerald green three-headed lizard out of the smoke with large leathery bat-like wings, a long whip-like tail, and strong clawed hind legs. Sitting on the ellén trechend, he sends a telepathic order to the beast his on. The trechend lunches forward, flying at the ray terror beast. It bites into the terror beast's side, pushing it away. Oran created a psychic shield around him and his mount, blocking them from its tail, lashing at them from across it. Every blow shoots out a burst of lighting, bouncing off the shield. It pushes it back in an arc, crashing into the forest, taking the brawl away from there so they can have more space to face their own terror beats.

The swift mantis beast rushes at Leifur at full speed, slicing at him wildly. Leifur leaps vertically across it, landing right on its abdomen. The mantis keeps running forward in between the trees, and its head turns around to look right at Leifur, smiling cockily at it. He jumps up in the air with his lute, playing a chord. Leifur sends a sound blast right at its face, sending it careening off. Leifur runs off after it, and the mantis gets back up on its legs, slicing at Leifur, who ducks underneath its slashes as he approaches. He plays the lute again, sending a sound blast upwards. Launching the mantis beast straight through the forest canopy, Leifur runs up a tree, pushing off a large branch, and throws himself after the terror beast.

Blaire sprints around the foot of the mountain with the eel terror beast pursuing her doggedly. Its deadly tendrils try to lash out at Blaire as it slithers behind her. Blaire opens a portal before her, leaping through it with the terror beast following behind. She then opens another portal, going through it with the beast following. She continues this, creating a new portal every meter until one of its tendrils snags her leg as she exited a portal, making her fall flat to the ground.

Blaire looks back at the swirling portal as its grim head looms from it, with a maw open showing rows of needle-sharp teeth. The incredible parts of its incredibly long body poke out of multiple portals placed across the area. Blaire looks at it. "Got you.… you slimy hideous brute !" She yells out with a big smile as she holds up her hand, closing her hand into a fist. As she does this, every portal she has created closes, slicing its entire body piece and falling to the ground... all around her. Blaire stands up, holding her hand to her side; she looks at her defeated foe's head smugly. "That's what you get for.… eek!" She screams as the eel terror beast's maw opens, screeching.

Blaire steps back in fear. Instinctively, she takes out her whip and cracks it at the head. It whips around the head, restraining its maw. Hastily, she takes out her dagger, stabbing it right between the eyes, slaying it. Blaire falls down next to the head, sitting back against it. She watches Fritz as he shoots off arrows with his crossbow at a bat terror beast while dodging the beast's ultra-sonic attacks.

Fritz hurriedly changed his arrows, using one with a bomb attached to the end, as he kept on the move so he wouldn't get hit by the beast's sound projectiles. He rolls away from an attack, firing back at the center of its body. It explodes into a fiery explosion, burning holes into its wings leathery wings, making it plummet to the ground. Fritz conjures a saber into each hand, running at the beast. His blades clash against the bat beast's long metal claws. Fritz spars with it, keeping up with its slashes and jabs. Fritz observes his opponent, considering his next move. He swiftly slices off one of the beast's arms, getting sliced by the beast's claws across his chest while doing it. Fritz ducks under an ultra-sonic counterattack, cutting the other arm as he leaps back up to his feat. Throwing his saber behind him, it disperses into purple smoke. He conjures a bastard sword, drives it through the beast's chest, and finishes the monster off.

Fritz pulls it out, letting the beast collapse on the ground. He throws his sword in the air, allowing it to disperse into smoke. Placing his hands behind his head in a relaxed posture. He looks to his side, jumping back to avoid Kamaria running incredibly fast past him with a trail of light, shooting light shards at the lighting-fast weasel terror beast chasing her.

Kamaria creates a blade of light, stopping in her tracks. She blocks the beast's claws as it lunges at her, pushing it forcefully away from her. She shoots out more at the beast; it dodges these projectiles mid-air, twisting and turning around it with its long body before landing on the ground. It lunges back at her, and she creates another blade of light in her other hand. Blocking it again, but with both blades, she pushes the beast back. It skids to a halt, and she creates light shards, shooting a barrage of projectiles at it. It dodges this, not noticing Kamaria dashing right at him until the last second. Its hard claws lengthen to block her light blade, and she creates multiple blades of light above his head. Catching it by surprise, all the shards shoot down on its body, piercing across its frame. Kamaria finishes the beast by decapitating it with both her light blades.

She walks back from it, looking in awe at the fallen headless beast. She smiles widely at it, excited to examine the terror beast's body, along with that of the chimera.… when everyone's battle with their beast is over and done.

Kaylan stands still in the center of a glade, keeping his ears perked up and his eyes completely shut.….. to listen intently for the slightest of sounds or movement in the environment. He has slammed his mind orb into the chameleon terror beast, making it flee into the forest. He pursued it here. It's camouflaged itself completely; it's practically invisible. It might be close to him or hiding among the trees. His ear turns to the right, and quickly, he steps back. Avoiding being hit by its tongue, shooting out at him.

Kaylan's shape shifts hastily into his wolf form, biting onto the tongue sticking to the ground. Holding desperately onto it... so it won't pull it back and keep it in place. He sends the mind orb flying straight off, across the tongue to the terror beast hiding in a tree. Slamming into the beast with a tremendous crack. It fell down with the top part of the tree. Kaylan let go of the tongue as it hit the ground. He changes back into his standard form and cautiously gazes at the beast beneath the tree. The long tongue from him to the beast suddenly retracts back into the terror beast's mouth, hitting Kaylan as it does.

The chameleon beast leaps out from the forest right over him, shooting out its tongue at Kaylan, to be stopped by the mind orb bursting out of the forest right into its path. It retracts its tongue, trying to leap over Kaylan again, only to be struck down by the mind orb bashing against its side. Sending it hurdling right down to the ground in a straight path. Crashing into a cloud of dust, dirt shooting out everywhere. A tongue shoots out of this, sticking on Kaylan's chest, pulling him slowly in as Kaylan holds tightly onto a root sticking out of the ground so he won't get dragged in. He sends his mind orb, now covered in a bright, sharp blue aura, flying up high in the sky, hurdling down. It slams into the terror beast's head, ramming it straight into the ground with full force... burying most of its body in the dirt.

Kaylan walks over to it, making sure it's down. Waiting a moment, he confirms it has been slain. "I did it...." Kaylan says under his breath, elated that he did it; he actually fought and won. Kaylan looks up happily. I hoped somehow that Conor could have seen this from the great beyond.

Fighting on the very top of the mountain, the blood chimera viciously slashes down at Atgeir with its claws, missing as Atgeir moves around the attack, punching at the chimera's chest with a barrage of electrified attack, bruising its body slightly. The chimera pulls back its head before breathing out a ball of fire at him. Atgeir blocks this with his gauntlets, pushed back a bit by the force of the blast. Atgeir covers the clawed tips of his gauntlets with his scarlet lighting, launching it at the chimera. The monster flinches in pain as it hits its face, scaring it slightly. Getting back his composure, he spins around. Using its long whip-like tail to slam into Atgeir's legs, making him fall flat on the ground backward. Atgeir rolls up from his back, leaping back to his feet with a powerful kick.

Atgeir lunges at the chimera, jabbing towards its throat, missing its hair as he tilts its head far to the side. The chimera claws upward towards Atgeir, only tearing his coat, as the prince quickly steps back from the attack. Atgeir throws a ball of electricity at its head, the chimera ducking under it. The projectile explodes against its antlers, breaking one of them off. The chimera stumbles back from the force of the blast, getting back its footing.

"Let's take this brawl.... to the sky... elf !" The chimera shouts, furious at this. The chimera whips its tails around Atgeir body like a rope, flapping its massive wings; he launches into the air, carrying Atgeir in its tails. Atgeir jabs at the tail with an electrified gauntlet while holding onto it with the other. The chimera screeches in pain, completely loosening the grip of its tail on him. Whipping Atgeir with his tail higher up into the air, the chimera shoots off a fireball at him. Atgeir dodges this mid-air, going down with an axe kick covered in his scarlet lightning. The chimera plummets down, right into the mountain's stone, with a tremendous impact. Shattering a large part of the mountain in a rain of boulders and rocks, falling down from it.

Atgeir closes his eyes momentarily, forming a crystallized-looking crimson spear out of his mana, enveloping the entire thing in lighting. He throws it down viciously with his full force. Shooting it down at blinding speeds right into the chimera's chest, piercing right through it with a thunderous crash.

Atgeir strengthens the invisible layer of armor surrounding him, bracing himself as he crashes down next to the slain chimera.

Shakily, Atgeir gets up, his entire vision obscured by a cloud of dust; he waves it away, making it clearer to see there. It slowly dissipates, revealing the slain Blood chimera on its back with a gaping hole in its chest. Atgeir grins at this, savoring in his victory. Atgeir quickly grabs hold of his right arm, which feels like it's burning in agony all over. That ultima spell packed a punch; it lived up to the name they gave it, the divine lighting spear….. Atgeir sits down, exhausted from that spell and in a bit of anguish. However, still, he's joyous and relieved that his quest is finally over. Now his head is clear…. his mind is now bizarrely clear, able to think everything that has happened through and think back to one specific thing from his past, a memory he chose to disregard till now, brought up by something a particular puca creature told him…. that he was too stubborn to remember till now. One he can't believe was brought back into his mind by the words of some creature…. whose name he can't even try to recall.

CHAPTER 29
It's over…..

Hanging on to the top of a large tree, far away from the mountain, Dark watches this all end with his incredible long-distance sight in his humanoid form. "He has failed…." He says unemotionally, stroking his chin. "No matter, there is always the backup plan…." The being known as Dark mutters to himself as he leaps from branch to branch till he reaches the ground. He strolls into the dark, dense forest, where little light seeps through the thick, leafy canopy above.

Dark sighs as he wanders off deeper into the depths of the forest. "My followers will gladly carry out the rest of the plan…. then he will come to help complete my….. grand plan." He says, grinning his jagged, toothy grin. His smoky robes envelop his entire body, swirling around violently.

The smoke turns into a sphere of black and yellow smoke, shrinking to a smaller size, and disperses into the air. All that remains to be revealed is his small rat-like form, which scampers even deeper into the forest, cackling wildly in a shrill tone. Filling the air with the sound of wicked laughter.

A hundred and nine years ago, in the Severne realm, Hyvits Palace.

Atgeir stands in the dimly lit hallway, most of his scars healed by his mother when he returned with his brother from their horrible encounter. They came back hoping to sneak in but were caught immediately by their father and mother in the act, scared and bleeding from their wounds. Their mother went to both of their sides. She mostly healed their cursed wounds across their bodies, with the scars on their faces…. which she was strangely unable to heal… then again, the sulfrens are the manifested wrath of the divines towards mortals. That rage will surely stay on the ones they injure in the shape of an unfading scar, a reminder of their hate…..

After Sia patches them up, she reluctantly leaves them to their father's rage for what they did. Atgeir is waiting next to a door, listening as his father loudly scolds Leifur inside the library.

"What were you thinking? You could have gotten yourself, and Atgeir killed!" Eilif yells down at Leifur, sitting on a chair beside a table, looking down to the floor. "How could you think you could just wander out into the forest and not get caught by a sulfren….. neither of you are even capable of dealing with a monster like that!" Eilif furiously expresses his concerns and fears. Leifur just shakes his head at these words. "I wouldn't have snuck out tonight if you just took us out with you…. to explore these exciting places and creatures, but you just won't because there, it's harder for you to control what happens." Leifur says stoically, looking up at his father with defiance radiating from him. "That isn't it, boy… you just can't help yourself than to go against me every chance you get." Eilif says, stroking back his hair with his fingers, frustrated at Leifur's attitude. "No, it is you…. aptus stone test, I got an enhancement. Yet, you made me focus on becoming a pyromancer, an elemental class… how much control are you going to take from my life, are you seriously going to decide everything for me!" Leifur says coldly, holding tightly onto the arms of the chair.

"As much as I need, Leifur. You know you had to uphold the tradition of there being one eclipse pyromancer in every generation of our family lineage and I'm going to make sure you will uphold that as the heir to the throne." Eilif angrily explains his stand on it. "You could have changed it or got Atgeir to learn your beloved pyromancy, but you just had to get me to be the one…. but I fixed that; I was already busy learning to use…. sound magic instead of focusing on what you, the entire time…. chose for me!" Leifur retorts, barely keeping himself from bursting out in a rage.

"That's what I get for being too lenient with you…. from now on, I'm going to be far stricter on you; keep a closer eye on what you're up to. Restrict what you do and where you go during the day; this can't stand any longer." Eilif says confidently, steadfast in his cruel sentence upon Leifur.

Glaring hatefully at his father, Leifur stands up without saying a word. Storming right out of the library, slamming the door behind him. "Where do you think you are going? We haven't finished talking!" Eilif shouts out furiously, slamming his fist on the table, cracking it in two by the force of the impact.

Atgeir listens from the hallway as his father tears up the room in a fit of rage. Shaking his head, Atgeir walks away to find Leifur, who ran past him just a moment ago. All the way to Leifur's room, where he finds his brother sitting down on his bed, slumped over. "I guess you heard all of that." Leifur says as he notices Atgeir coming in. He just nods yes at the statement of fact. He sits down on the other side of the bed. "I can't…. I can't just let him do this to me. I have to…" Leifur says, feeling humiliated and defeated. "Father should have focused his attention on me instead of you… you don't get how great it is to be taught by someone as great as him…." Atgeir says, stopping as he looks over to see Leifur watching him sadly. "I guess that's right for you… but not for me…. definitely not for me... for me that's just a cage." Leifur says in a sorrowful tone, turning away from Atgeir.

Having vanquished the Blood Chimera and its horde, they immediately returned to Fort Borage, closer to the realm gate.

In the fort's courtyard, Oran stands beside Kaylan and Kamaria, sitting at a table; both are listening intently to him, with Blaire and Fritz standing further away, watching them. They are all holding a glass of cider in celebration. Strangely, though, Atgeir and his brother are entirely absent. "The great Blood Chimera is long gone; now we just need to dispose of the remainder of its terror beasts. This invasion will be over in almost no time at all." Oran tells them, celebrating their win over the Blood Chimera while confidently reaching an indelibly swift victory. "That will leave us to deal with the dead Chimera's body to examine and discover its secrets and where it came from." Kamaria adds, exited by the prospect.

"And after I have report our success to the king, we can do that. The arcane court is under his authority, so he should be informed as soon as possible." Oran brings up protocol, dampening Kaylan's enthusiasm a tad. "As I suspected, that will leave us more time to speculate and come up with some theories before we can really dissect the monster." Kamaria confidently says, assured it won't take that long for Oran to do what he must. "Perfectly said, my dear. I already concocted a couple of theories myself. I am certain it has ties to the fallen divines." Oran agrees entirely, raising his glass. Enthusiastic for whatever is to come and what they will all uncover.

"What are you band of brainy bookworms all talking about. Didn't you call us all here to celebrate our victory?" Fritz shouts out as he swaggers over to them. "This doesn't feel very lively. The drinks are nice, but I was hoping for something more." He cheerfully says, with a glass of ale in each hand. "Yeah, where's the big party !" Blaire chips in, walking out from behind him, holding her fist up. "Hold on, you two." Oran says, holding up his hand toward the rowdy duo. "I thought a more subdued celebration was in order after all that occurred. You two can go to the kitchen and celebrate as wildly as you see fit if that is what you wish." He tells them, laying his law down. "Sounds fine…. still wouldn't it be better if all three of you joined us. I sure know how to celebrate; you'll be missing out." Fritz says, trying to get them to come along.

"Thanks, but we'd rather decline. It isn't our style of commemorating our victories; we brainy bookworms, as you call us. Enjoy more peaceful celebrations." Kamaria speaks up to Fritz, leaning over the table.

Leaning back with his arms crossed behind his head, Fritz gives a cheeky smile. "Fine….. It's your loss. That will just leave more for me and B to enjoy." He says, grabbing Blaire's hand. "Yea, your so going to regret this!" she smugly adds as Fritz leads her away, laughing back at them. "See you later, Kam!" Fritz shouts as he disappears into the building. Leaving them to converse peacefully without any more interference and laying out their plans for what's to come.

Away from the members of the Arcane regiment and high above the fort, right on top of it. Atgeir and Leifur stand on top of a tower's roof, looking at the setting sun with a strong breeze blowing through the air. "You brought me up here; what do you want to say to me, Geir ?" Leifur asks, looking back at Atgeir. "I have been thinking about why you even left." Atgeir says in thought, carefully considering his words as now he fears losing his brother forever. He takes a moment, thinking things through again, and then he says what he came here for, having brought himself to do it.

"I finally realized you would never have been happy back home in the Severne realm… not with all the daily restrictions and limitations you must submit to. I don't really care about being able to explore the other realm, free of responsibilities." Atgeir says, gesturing slightly as he explains it. "For I love power and prestige and will do anything to keep and achieve greater heights, but you want to explore and go on treacherous adventures, unbound by duty…. I…. apologize for what… I said that night before…. you left, I was kind…. of wrong…." Atgeir finishes what he wants to say, struggling to say the last couple of words, as he isn't really one to apologize to anyone…. accepting his wrong. Having spent these last few days with his brother, he remembered how much he actually cared and respected his brother, and now he wants to keep him in his life.

Leifur smiles warmly at him. "Never thought I'd hear you say that, thank you." He says, walking up to Atgeir. He hugs him… catching Atgeir by surprise. Atgeir slowly embraces the hug before they let go of each other. "Just don't get used to it, brother. You won't get another apology out of me anytime soon…. besides with you gone, the throne is mine without a challenge…. I'm getting used to that great idea." Atgeir says smugly with a grin. "I suspected you'd say that, Geir… I guess that means we're going to have a future match." Leifur tells him back, chuckling at the notion. "Of course we will, I won't miss a chance at beating you in a fight." Atgeir responds laughing alongside him.

They let go of each other and return to the tranquil sunset, content with their newfound understanding. "I think things will become much better… in time." Leifur says calmly.

Walking along a path surrounded by the forest's trees at night, Atgeir, along with Leifur, Kaylan, and Kamaria, make their way to the realm gate; now, there is nothing left for Atgeir to do in this realm anymore. "Doesn't this feel a bit too easy?" Kaylan asks Kamaria as they walk. Looking back on the entirety of the quest to slay the blood chimera. "What do you mean by that?" She answers his question with another, confused by his statement. "Me and Atgeir running to each other as he just enters the realm…. the chimera making itself known in the village so we can find him… And so forth, it just feels like something was orchestrating it." Kaylan responds, trying to piece something together.

"Don't overthink it, creature. I came out victorious in this, and that's all that matters." Atgeir says back to them smugly. "I know it is in the past and well done and over, but still, there has to be more to it." Kaylan defends his stance on this. "Better not bother the prince. Remember, we can just discover things when he's gone." Kamaria says, placing her arm around his shoulders. Kaylan blushes at this, getting flustered. He looks away from her quickly, hiding his face from her. "That's…. sounds…. like an excellent plan." He says timidly.

They walk up to the realm gate, looking at the large jade structure. Atgeir turns around, looking at Leifur. "I guess this means goodbye." He says, holding out his hand. "It is for now; maybe we'll figure it out so I can show Mother I'm alive while not letting Father know. Just need to get her to keep it a secret." Leifur says cheerfully, shaking his outstretched hand. "Sounds perfect." Atgeir says before he goes over to Kaylan, hopeful they can get what they both want in the near future. Taking a deep breath, Atgeir talks to him. "Creature … thanks… for helping… sort of repairing me and my brother's…. bond, I could have done it myself, but you helped…. I guess." Atgeir says, struggling to say each word to this creature he sees beneath him, that he doesn't even bother remembering its name…. trying not to sound too grateful for his help. Kaylan looks at him in disbelief as Atgeir, with Kamaria next to him, giggles at this sight; they watch as he speedily turns around. He goes to the pedestal to place his traveler's stone in the slot so he can escape this uncomfortable situation through the portal.

He places the disc in the slot, and it suddenly makes a crackling sound as green sparks fly from it. Bursting in a small explosion of smoke, it shatters to pieces, only a tiny light flickering in the gate before it vanishes. Atgeir looks down at the broken traveler's disc in a rush of fear and confusion. "That's not supposed to happen." Leifur says, leaning over the pedestal to look at it. Atgeir picks up the fragments of the shattered traveler's stone, unsure what to do now. He looks back over at his brother. "Wait!…. I think I still have mine with me….. somewhere." Leifur says as he digs through his pockets, looking for his traveler's stone and looking in his pouches, finding it nowhere. Unsuccessful at finding it, Leifur looks back up at him. "Sorry, I can't find it. It was there a moment ago…. I don't know." He tries to explain to Atgeir, holding his hands up to his sides and shrugging. Atgeir watches this in horror; he can't get back to his realm. This can't be it; how did this happen? Did Thyra give him a faulty traveler's stone on purpose…. did she know about it…. still there is one thing he does know, he has to find a new stone, or he'll end up stuck in this realm forever.

Back in the Severne realm, Hyvits palace.

Sitting around a long, dark wooden dining table adorned with golden and silver patterning in a grand hall, Eilif sits with his family eating dinner. A small intricate dish made of sliced vegetables and meat circles stacked neatly on each other and refreshing cordial poured in each one's glass, the room lit up by silver chandeliers, its candles alight with blue flames. Sia, next to Eilif, looked down at her plate nervously. She looks up at her husband in concern, before turning her gaze back to her plate.

Sia proceeds to anxiously plays around with the fabric of her dress underneath the table. Listening to Aada talking about how her day went to Eilif. Sia's visage, showing all her anxiety and despair to everyone, was no longer hidden. "Is something wrong, Si ?" Eilif asks comfortingly at her.

The tension... the tension within her rises at his voice.... higher and higher.... until she can't any longer... until...

She suddenly breaks at this. "Atgeir is gone; he left and has been gone for over two weeks. He's not at the defense towers.... he's gone to prove something, on some dangerous quest !" She yells out frantically, tearing up as she says it.

Eilif pulls away from her, taken aback. "Did you just say..... Atgeir has been gone for this long.... and now you tell me." Eilif says, appalled, horrible thoughts racing through his head, on what could have happened to Atgeir, why he isn't back yet, why nobody told him till then, will he lose his last son.... no, it can't be.

They all are freaking out over this terrible predicament.... while Thyra just sits all the way on the other side of the table, away from them. Watching her family with a wicked smile slowly spreading across her face.

EPILOGUE
Radiant knights brotherhood

In the Thiar realm, the pale moonlight dances across a sandy shore. Behind the illuminated beach, a large cliff face looms, with the gentle sounds of waves crashing against the clusters of enormous rocks dotted along the strand. A large glowing white portal opens up above the sand, and a young man leaps out of it. His scarlet eyes carefully looked back and forth along the shore for any threats. He is wearing a blue tunic with a coat of arms on it depicting a large, stylized rose embroidered on a thorny vine-covered shield design with two wyverns posed to the sides of it. Under the tunic, he wears a long-sleeved chain mail shirt with a spatha sword made of green divine metal and a black arfvedsonite on the end of the hilt hanging on his belt. He looks back at the portal, having concluded there are no threats. The portal's glow makes his pale face look even paler as he strokes back his brown hair, strangely styled to resemble horns. "Sir Lannigan, it's clear!" He yells out to someone unseen within the portal.

A strong-looking man leaps out, wearing a suit of armor with a long red cape with his heraldry on it: a three-headed dragon over two crossed swords that lay upon a kite shield. He has short, neat black hair covered by a hood. The knight is followed by two other men. Quite Identical in appearance, one wearing a leopard pelt as a cloak and the other the skin of a crocodile - the first wears a patterned black robe, and the second a white one. Their dark-skinned faces are painted with intricate red markings, while a metal mask resembling the coat of the beast each is wearing hangs on each of their belts - the leopard having a red beryl embedded in its mask, and the other a tsavorite garnet. "We're finally back home, Grendel. The Radiant Knights brotherhood has returned to its land." Sir Lannigan says enthusiastically. He looks around, taking in the surroundings with his grey eyes, having been gone for a year in a pocket realm, honing their skills, away from distractions. The other knights slowly start coming out of the portal, marching across the shore. "Can't wait to get out there and get back to business, Sir Lannigan." Aziz the leopard says, taking a deep breath of the cold predawn air. "We are itching for a real fight - all scoundrels shall tremble at seeing our return." Jabari, the crocodile adds, grinning widely. "Both of your enthusiasms are admirable, but now is not the time; we haven't even settled back into our fortress yet." Grendel tells them sternly.

The twins just chuckle loudly at this. "We all just arrived back, and you're already ordering us around." Aziz remarks through his laughter, stroking back his long dreadlocks. "You never change, do you Grendel? Always so strict and commanding." Jabari chips in, smirking mischievously at him. "And neither of you can take anything seriously…" Grendel snaps back, stopped by Sir Lannigan. "This is not the time for arguing; there are far more important things to attend to." He silences the three knights.

Sensing the tension, the twins gaze at each other, nodding in agreement at what they have to do. They Walk away from this conversation further along the shoreline, leaving them to the matter they have to discuss. Grendel walks closer to his master. "What is the matter, Sir Lannigan." He senses something amiss in the master knight.

"I was just wondering if our dear realm has been invaded or sent into chaos by a threat within…. in our absence. There could be a great conflict waiting for us." Sir Lannigan says, looking over to Grendel. "Why would anyone do that, with it being well known that the realm is under our very protection. They wouldn't have known we were gone on their decennial outing this year." Grendel responds adamantly. "I hope so… yet something does feel wrong in the world, like a large loss of life." Sir Lannigan says, weary of the state of the realm. There is trouble coming. There is a mighty fight ahead. Tension mounts and he can only imagine the next days' horrors. Time will tell…

Components of Arcane Weapons
Metal Ores

Used to forge your weapon of choice
The metal conducts mana through it to cast stronger spells

Metal	Best suited for		Unique attribute
Steel	Enhancement Fortitude Might Strenghtener	Transformation Size-Changer	enhances wielders resilience
Brass	Elemental Geomancy	Enhancement Might Strenghtener	enhances strenght and can shoot out strong shockwaves
copper	Mind All branches besides healing Mind control and premonition	Elemental Electromancy Ilumimancy	Strenghtens range of mind class spells
Black Steel	enhancement accelerater Fortitude Vision Ehancement	Transformation Identity Stealer	Increase wielders speed Can hide your mana presence
Bronze	Elemental Floramancy	Enhancement Enhance hearing	Draws small amounts of mana from around it
Titanium	Mind Healing	Transformation Transmutation Shape-Shifting	Decrease mana use slightly
Platinum	Elemental Zephyrmancy Illumimancy	Mind Premonition Mind control	Can better sense mana pressences
Silver	Elemental Cryomancy Hydromancy	Mind Healing Telekinesis	Regains used mana slowly during battle
Gold	Elemental Pyromancy Illumimancy Electromancy	Mind Telekinesis Premonition	strenghtens spells even more
Divine metal	Reality All branches of class	Mind All branches of class	Decrease mana use and can rega mana slowly during battle

Components of Arcane Weapons
Gems

Gets embedded into the weapon of choice
Enhances and slightly alters the spells different ways

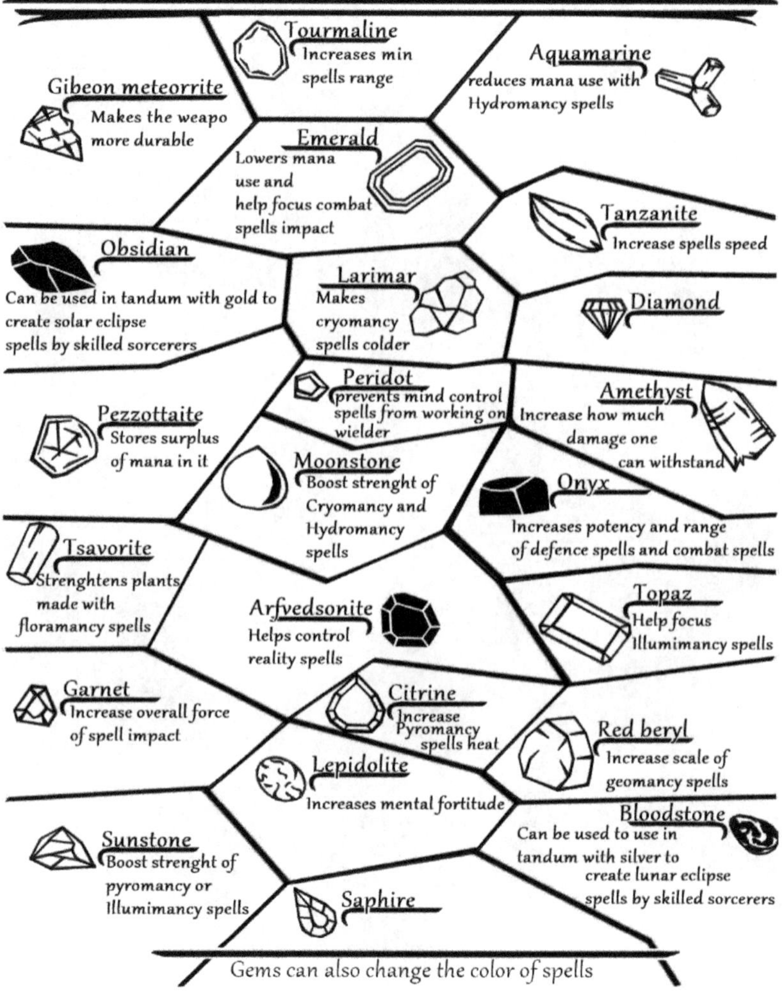

Gems can also change the color of spells

ABOUT THE AUTHOR

Bianca Taylor

Bianca Taylor is a fresh young addition to the fantasy literary genre. She is a creative artist with a passion for an enchanting tale, in both the literary and visual arts. She delights in inviting other readers into her world with characters she thoughtfully created. Having worked a bit on the site, Webtoon on an incomplete comic, a small story that will influence the making of Silver Chronicles, after realizing she wasn't the best at drawing. Having moved from place to place in her childhood from small towns to cities, till she finally found settled in one place. Bianca lives in the historic city of Kimberley, South Africa. Writing a beautifully expansive story in Silver Chronicles.